A POISON SPREADS: JACK SEEKS THE ANTIDOTE

ALSO BY MARK GREATHOUSE

The Frontier Chronicles

Perilous Trails: Jack's Adventure Begins

Wyoming Calls: Jack's Risky Quest

Longhorns North: Jack's Great Trail Drive

Warpath: Jack's Faith is Tested

Hunter Vs. Hunted: Jack's Great Frontier Challenge

Freedom Drovers: Jack's Awesome Crusade

The Tumbleweed Sagas

Nueces Justice

Nueces Reprise

Nueces Deceit

Nueces Blood

Nueces Grit

Nueces Truth

Nueces Legend

A POISON SPREADS: JACK SEEKS THE ANTIDOTE

THE FRONTIER CHRONICLES
BOOK 7

MARK GREATHOUSE

WISE WOLF
BOOKS

A Poison Spreads: Jack Seeks the Antidote

Paperback Edition
Copyright © 2025 by Mark Greathouse

WISE WOLF BOOKS
An Imprint of Wolfpack Publishing
1707 E. Diana Street
Tampa, FL 33610

wisewolfbooks.com

Paperback ISBN 978-1-965596-05-0
eBook ISBN 978-1-965596-04-3
LCCN 2025936028

Dedicated with love to my wife Carolyn, our two sons Mike and Matt, and the memory of my father John F. (Jack) Greathouse

"For their vine is from the vine of Sodom, and from the fields of Gomorrah; their grapes are grapes of poison, their clusters, bitter."

DEUTERONOMY 32:32

JACK'S UNDERGROUND RAILROAD

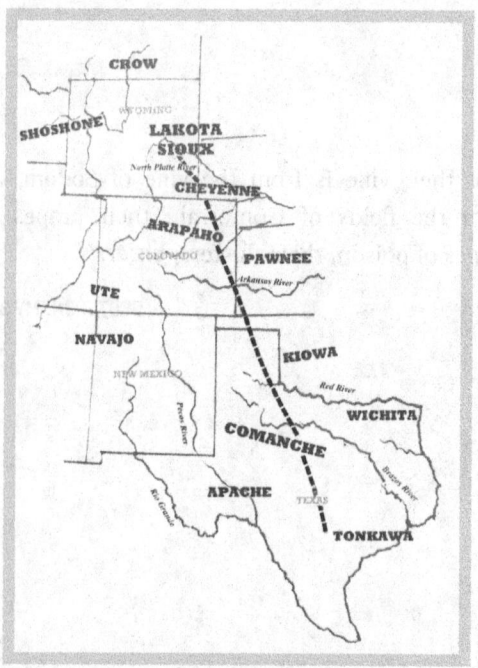

Route used by Jack and Spirit Talker in sneaking escaped slaves northward from Texas to Wyoming. It featured challenging landscapes and many tribes known to be hostile. Notably, it followed the Western Trail eventually used for great cattle drives. (Map by Mark Greathouse)

YOU ARE INVITED

Dear Reader,

If you've read *Perilous Trails, Wyoming Calls, Longhorns North, Warpath, Hunter Vs. Hunted,* and *Freedom Drovers,* it's likely my story has fully grabbed you. Obviously, I survived the attempted lynching. This seventh part of my tale is set in 1860. You recall that back in 1855, I had been thrown alone and vulnerable onto the vast Comancheria, made dangerous by the predations against White settlers by Comanche and Kiowa. I am now twenty years old. I've journeyed four times to Wyoming, first exploring the trail northward, twice driving herds of longhorns to my friend George Freeman's ranch on the North Platte, and once escaping threats to my family. Hostilities between Whites and Indians had exploded, and slavery was a huge issue. There was a poison spreading throughout the nation.

A Poison Spreads: Jack Seeks the Antidote continues the tales of my frontier adventures, further testing my courage, faith, endurance, pure grit, and—now—a mission. The Indians now call me Walks With Wolves.

The journeys to the North Platte sure taught me a ton more of life lessons. Do keep in mind that my story incorporates history not found in most school history books. This book relates my tale as driven by fate and guided by God.

I have met up with plenty of Indians, especially Comanche and Lakota Sioux, so you'll find me using some of their language throughout *Freedom Drovers*. I have provided a handy glossary of Comanche and Lakota words toward the back of this book.

I'm a Christian, but I have tried to grasp the Comanche and Lakota religions to better understand them. The Indian religion is based upon what is referred to as animism in which every common natural item from fish and animals to plants, trees, waterways, and mountains were believed to have souls or spirits. The spirits and traditions connected with them guided the Comanche and Lakota. Their passion for their spirits no doubt gave them their fearlessness as fed by the belief that they were protected in everything they did. Would they kill to defend their beliefs? Theirs was not a religion of love and forgiveness.

Could Indians like the Comanche or Lakota become Christians? My story in *Freedom Drovers* continues my evolution at the intersection of faith and culture. It was like Saint Patrick's conversion of the Irish to Christianity by folding many of their less-offensive heathen rites into the Catholic faith. Would this work with the Indians? Well, it's part of the story I'm sharing with y'all.

As you follow my adventures, ask yourself whether you might be up to meeting the challenges I take on. Dangers? Privations? Hmmm. How might you have fared? Through it all, I first relied on the teachings from my family, then went on to learn from the raw and risky experiences I faced. I learned to trust in instincts forged from my biblical lessons.

To be straight here, I had no idea that my story was going to fill multiple volumes until I began to write it all down. I invite you to follow my adventures on America's western frontier.

Kindest regards,
John *Jack* O'Toole

THE CAST

Jack O'Toole—*Twenty-year-old son of Joseph and Anna O'Toole. He strives to carve a life from the Texas frontier on the easternmost reaches of the Comancheria. Earned Comanche name Isa Pohya, Walks With Wolves.*

Mukwooru (a.k.a., Spirit Talker)—*Twenty-year-old son of a Penateka Comanche chief camped within the heart of the Comancheria. The warrior name bestowed upon teen Wild Horse in recognition of his apparent connection with Taa Narumi (the Comanche Great Father) whom they confused with God.*

Blue Flower—*Young sister to Spirit Talker and daughter to Buffalo Hump, she's married to Jack. They have three young children, George, Isa, and Peter.*

George Freeman—*A Black cowboy driving cattle north, later an Army scout. He establishes a ranch on the North Platte River in Wyoming.*

Running Waters—*George Freeman's Pawnee wife.*

Kate—*Jack's sixteen-year-old sister now married to Will Smith.*

Buck—*Jack's thirteen-year-old brother.*

Isaac Fisher—*An Amish farmer from Pennsylvania seeking new opportunities on the frontier.*

Sarah Fisher—*Isaac Fisher's wife and mother to baby son named Jack.*

Topsannah (a.k.a., Prairie Flower)—*Young Comanche girl captured and enslaved by Arapaho Lived on George Freeman's ranch. Marries Spirit Talker.*

Sam Collins—*Owner of the Circle C Ranch located near Jack's spread.*

Hank Johnson—*Cowhand on Collins's Circle C Ranch.*

Juan Perez—*Creative, hard-nosed Mexican cook on Jack's trail drive.*

Shorty McBride—*Drover on Jack's Crusade who lives up to his nickname.*

Willard Will Smith—*First hired hand on the Rising Cross Ranch. He marries Kate O'Toole.*

Stella Klappenbach—*August Klappenbach's wife.*

Hardy Sullivan—*Grizzled Texas Ranger who becomes friends with Jack and finds God.*

William McGregor—*A Scottish immigrant who serves as blacksmith and pastor in Austin, TX.*

Colleen McGregor—*William McGregor's wife.*

Zeb (Zebadiah)—*A wolf the Jack believes is a gift from God. They develop an ever-closer bond as the Frontier Chronicles evolve.*

Reginald Wilson IV—*Legacy nephew of Sarah Fisher sent west to learn how to be a man.*

Brawny Jones—*Slave catcher living from the bounties of captured slaves.*

Gordon Small—*Newspaper reporter on assignment to write stories about the frontier for eastern readers.*

Rolf Schultz—*Pro-slavery rabble-rouser from back east who is out to stop abolitionists.*

Cutter Kincaid—*Elfin hermit-like survivor of life who helps abolitionists.*

James—*Escaped slave who joins Jack's second underground railroad trail drive.*

Frederick—*Escaped slave who joins Jack's second underground railroad trail drive.*

Sheesha—*Escaped woman slave who seeks to become a cowpoke. Frederick's close friend.*

Colt Crockett—*Wrangler for Sam Collins's Circle C Ranch and friend to Jack O'Toole.*

Burt Colthwaite—*Texas plantation owner with a reputation for mistreating slaves.*

Samuel—*Indentured servant whom Jack rescues from a maniacal plantation owner.*

―――

HISTORICAL CHARACTERS

Hardin Richard Runnels—*Sixth governor of the state of Texas, slave owner.*

Sam Houston—*Leader of Texas independence, first president of Texas, leads them to statehood, serves as governor and US Senator.*

Buffalo Hump—*War chief of the Penateka Comanche, the southernmost band of the Comanche people in the Comancheria. In the famous Council House Fight of 1840, he led roughly a thousand Comanche across Texas to the Gulf Coast where they ransacked Victoria and burned Linnville.*

Captain Nathan Benton—*Texas Ranger captain assigned to protect settlers from Indians in the Leona River region northwest of Fort Inge near present-day Uvalde. (Benton eventually would serve as a lieutenant colonel in the Confederate Army, 36th Texas Cavalry.)*

Tasunke Witko (a.k.a. Crazy Horse)—*Future chief of Oglala Lakota of the Sioux Nation. He is about 19 years old at the time of this story, but already gaining attention of tribal leaders. He will go on to lead the massacre of General Custer's troops at Little Big Horn (a.k.a., Greasy Grass) in 1876.*

Tatanka Iyotake (a.k.a. Sitting Bull)—*Chief and medicine man of Hunkpapa band of Lakota Sioux.*

August Klappenbach—*Early settler of Bandera, TX and owner of first general store and post office.*

Thomas Twiss—*Indian agent assigned to Fort Laramie region.*

John Salmon Rip Ford—*Texas Ranger, doctor, lawyer, journalist, newspaper owner, legislator, and eventual Confederate colonel.*

Quanah Parker—*Eventual chief of the Quahadi band of the Comanche nation. Son of Comanche Chief Peta Nocona and White captive Cynthia Ann Parker.*

Alexander Hoffman—*Sheriff of Bandera County from 1856 to early 1860. Killed by Indians near Uvalde, Texas in March 1860.*

A POISON SPREADS: JACK SEEKS THE ANTIDOTE

PROLOGUE

HOW HAD I let this happen? A cardinal rule on the frontier is to never ever let your guard down. Ride just about anywhere on its rough and tumble vastness, and death could be waiting around the next bend in the trail. You had to be ever watchful. I had taken this early-morning ride by myself—much to Blue Flower's concern—to think on the future, especially mine. We had just purchased the Carlson spread north of the Guadalupe River. I had been gazing in deep thought across the river and up into the beautiful trees that lined its banks, when a grizzled voice challenged me to surrender and eight heavily armed men back up the voice. I expect they would be called vigilantes. They made short work of disarming me, tying my hands behind my back, and fashioning a lynch knot which they were pleased to loop around my neck and tighten. They figured to make Big Red take off and leave me dangling from a cypress branch. But my beloved stallion wouldn't budge, even when struck hard by a grizzled voice's hand. So, they yanked me from my horse and sat me on a smaller gelding. I was sweating despite the chill morning air.

Despite my dire circumstances, I found myself trying to recognize my attackers. One in particular caught my eye—not that it especially mattered at this instance in time. The rider was well off away from the necktie party, sort of like an observer. He wore a black hat and mask that covered most of his face, but most notable was the unusual black tack on his black stallion. The stallion had one white forelock. If by some slim chance I survived, I'd never forget the image. It was evil incarnate.

Big Red and I spoke a silent language. Once I was out of his saddle, he took off toward the Rising Cross Ranch house. Not that it would do any good. Here I sat aboard a skittish gelding with a rope around my neck that was tied off to the cypress trunk. Eight heavily armed and masked men laughed and carried on as they sat their saddles to witness my certain demise. They called me all manner of names while accusing me of being a *Negra lover* and slave runner. They mixed in some vile expletives. I thought I recognized a couple of the voices, but I'd have been hard-pressed to identify any of them were I to escape. The gnarly character with the grizzled voice that was also vaguely familiar to me was about to slap the rump of the gelding and let the rope strangle me to death.

Zeb watched nearby on high alert, awaiting an opportunity to help me. Was my Lord watching this? Where was my God when I needed Him?

There, I was about as vulnerable as any man could possibly be. What goes through any man's mind as he faces death? Did I think of my beloved Blue Flower? My family? My friends? To tell the truth, I was simply scared and praying to God like my life depended on it. It was.

Then, a shot rang out.

ONE
RESCUE

A HOLE APPEARED dead center between the startled eyes of grizzled voice. In the same instant, Zeb leaped and thudded full force onto the dying man's back. His jaws fastened with crushing force on the man's neck. They fell to earth together.

The gelding sprang forward. The tree branch bent under my weight, though I found myself momentarily hanging by my neck until I regained my balance and could stand precariously on my tiptoes.

A second shot blasted from the riverbank, and one of the vigilantes fell from his saddle. A third shot unhorsed another misguided soul.

"Let's git outta here!" hollered one of the vigilantes.

In but a heartbeat, a knife had sliced the rope. "Yuh sure 'nuf find trouble, Mr. O'Toole."

I opened my eyes to find myself staring into those of Brawny Jones. What was he doing here now at this very moment in time when he was needed most? The man I'd shown mercy to three times had returned to repay me big time! I gave him a hug from which he quickly wrestled free.

"Don't get carried away, O'Toole!" he advised with a smile.

The sound of approaching hoofbeats grabbed our attention. Shorty, Hardy, Will, and even young Buck came charging in at full gallop. I shouldn't have been surprised, as Blue Flower rode with them. She had Big Red in tow. They arrived in a cloud of prairie dust. Blue Flower flew from her mare and into my arms.

Other than rope burns on my neck and wrists, I was none the worse for wear. It sure felt good to be embracing the woman I feared I might never again see. Her head buried in my chest was more than enough to remind me of all I held dear.

"Kahni…kamakuna…kahni…kamakuna…Taa Narumi." The words flowed gently, lovingly from her quivering lips. Life, love, and God were the very heartbeat of life. She had nearly lost me. I didn't grasp it at the time, but upon reflection, this moment cemented my decision to stay close to home, to my wife, children and family.

The men dismounted and began yanking bandannas from the faces of the dead vigilantes. Brawny recognized the grizzled voice as a former partner in his slave catcher business. The man had been killed by Brawny's head shot but was a mess, given that he was nearly beheaded by Zeb. Two of the vigilantes turned out to be cowboys from a spread south of Rising Cross Ranch. The third vigilante that had fallen to Brawny's marksmanship skills was no one any of us recognized. Importantly, he was seriously wounded but not so badly as to be on death's doorstep.

We propped the wounded man against the base of the

cypress that—ironically—was to serve as the hanging tree.

I kissed Blue Flower and eased over to the wounded man. There was business to tend to.

Brawny was still catching his breath. He'd run full tilt to me with knife in hand to cut the devil's rope from my neck. "What do you think, Mr. O'Toole?" he asked.

I put my hand aside my mouth to shield my words from the wounded man and turned to Brawny. "We need to find out who organized this necktie party." I desperately wanted to ask Brawny why he'd returned. That would have to wait. "Somebody sent these ne'er-do-wells."

"It be easy these days to work folks to a lather," observed Brawny. "Folks lose their heads."

Shorty joined us. "Yer friend Spirit Talker would know what to do, boss."

I nodded and drew my Bowie knife. "I hear tell Apache scalp folks while they live."

The wounded man looked up pleadingly. He winced with pain from the wound in his side that made it difficult to breathe. "No...for the love of God, no," he pleaded.

Blue Flower grabbed my knife-wielding hand. "Make mess," she said, shaking her head with a grimness. She gave me a hurry-home look and turned to her mare. "I go home. Make coffee," she said as though she'd resolved any thoughts of my scalping the wounded vigilante.

I turned to Brawny and Shorty. "She's right. I don't think I can keep myself from carving this man's heart out. You find who he is and who sent him." With that, I sheathed my knife, spat at the wounded vigilante, and headed home on Big Red with Zeb tailing behind. As I rode away, I could hear the relieved vigilante confessing, spilling his guts as to the lynching.

Shorty knocked on our cabin door about an hour later.

"Come on in," I called.

Blue Flower had set coffee and bear sign on the table, and the men needed no arm-twisting to dig in.

"We buried them best we could, boss. Grabbed their personal effects." With that, he produced a leather sack that he passed to me. I gulped. I wasn't looking forward to returning these items to the ranches that spawned the vigilantes.

"Who was the wounded man?"

"Don Strong from the Running Bar spread. He did pass away from his wound," reported Shorty. He sounded relieved.

I had spoken with the owner of the Running Bar and thought we'd reached a truce on the slavery issue. "Did he say who organized the necktie party?"

"Dude from New Orleans name of Rolf Schultz been stirrin' folks up in Bandera. Figure Schultz be a coward, as he din't ride with the vigilantes," reported Brawny, who paused and looked around the room. "Some newspaper fella named Small was writin' about it—stirrin' things up. Them writer folks'll say most anythin' to sell papers," he observed.

"What do you propose we do?" asked Hardy, turning to me. I could sense his Texas Ranger experience kicking in.

It seemed that every decision eventually wound up in my lap. I guess me, Pohya Isa, Walks With Wolves, had become the designated leader of the pack. What could I do but accept? Someone had to or all would be lost. I was the one who constantly strove upward, reflected the truth, and offered a future of achieving noble, God-driven ends. Just as Abraham in the Old Testament was called upon to leave the comforts of home to take on a world fallen into sin, I was being called to help us rise above our circumstances. In the years since the Comanche attack on my family, I had already recognized that the risks taken in adventure are absolute, given the undeniable and ever-present reality of death and evil. That I trusted in God to face them was a testament to my faith and to the deep faith, hopes, and convictions of those I led. As my Comanche brother Spirit Talker had so often assured me, I held strong *sunipu* blessed upon me by God. My wolf companion Zeb was further testament to His will. A poison—slavery—was spreading throughout the nation, and I was being called to seek the antidote. "We'll face up to it," I said emphatically. "We'll take the bull by the horns. We'll fight against those who turn to violence to preserve their misguided, fear-driven support of slavery." With that, I turned to Brawny to ask the question that had been burning in my mind since he saved me from the vigilantes. "What brought you back?"

Brawny hung his head in a sheep-doggish aw-shucks manner, then looked me square in the eyes. "Started readin' thet Good Book yuh gave me. Din't git them ye's an' thee's an' thou's too well, but it made sense. I seen the error of my ways."

"You don't figure to catch slaves anymore?" I asked almost rhetorically.

"Better then thet, Mr. O'Toole," he responded. "I be hoping to find a job with yuh."

I glanced at Shorty and Hardy. They nodded. "Well, load your gear in the bunkhouse, Brawny. Welcome to Rising Cross Ranch." I reckoned I'd made a true believer. With vigilantes and hostile Indians to contend with on a growing ranch, another hand that could shoot straight was welcome. Now came the matter of dealing with the vigilantes. If they could single me out, then my family and friends were at risk. I knew that Rip Ford and his Texas Rangers were taking on a Mexican rebel named Juan Cortina down on the Rio Grande. I couldn't be certain which side of the slavery question Bandera Sheriff Alexander Hoffman was on. A man wearing the badge was supposed to uphold the law regardless of politics. "Guess I'll be heading to Bandera," I said with resignation. "Figure to enlist Sheriff Hoffman to help deliver these personal effects."

"What about Schultz, boss?" reminded Hardy.

"Mebbe a couple of us should go with yuh," suggested Shorty.

I nodded. Going it alone would have been downright risky. I had to think of my family. I looked over at Blue Flower.

She knew that I had to take care of the matter were there to be any hope of a peaceful life here in Texas. "You must go," she said with just a hint of reluctance in her voice. One of the laws of the frontier was often having to do things that entailed risk for a greater good.

It occurred to me that Spirit Talker might visit for Christmas. That would be welcome, as I would entrust watching over his sister while I dealt with matters in Bandera. I stood. "Let's get this over with. Shorty, Hardy, and Brawny come with me to Bandera. We'll leave tomorrow morning." Inwardly, I was praying to God that all would go well.

Blue Flower smiled.

As the men headed to the bunkhouse, I found myself thinking on Brawny Jones. The now-reformed slave catcher had attacked me and my men three times. We defeated him each and every time. I'd shown mercy twice and let him go, albeit with no weapons or horses...or clothes. On the third time, I sent him off with a Bible and promise that he'd better never cross me again. Now, he'd returned and was responsible for saving my life. God sure worked in strange ways.

TWO
BANDERA

WE RODE out soon after sunup. Blue Flower had fixed a fine breakfast for me, and Perez had fed the men at the bunkhouse. Will and Kate stopped by to see us off, and Buck promised to care for the livestock best he could, though he clearly wished he was going with us. Buck had just turned eleven but saw himself as grown up after having joined us on the trail drive to the North Platte country. I had hoped that Spirit Talker and Prairie Flower might visit, but time was wasting and we had to get on with the distasteful task of returning the vigilantes' personal effects and reporting the assault on me.

The air was chillier than most December mornings in the hills of Central Texas. We sure as shooting didn't look forward to crossing the frigid through shallow waters of the Medina River, not once, but twice. I must admit to feeling a certain sense of security with Shorty, Hardy, and Brawny accompanying me. Zeb trotted along in our rear. We were heavily armed with rifles, revolvers, our trusty Bowie knives, and plenty of ammunition. I even brought along my Comanche-style bow with a quiver of arrows. I'm not sure what possessed me to carry what I mentally referred to as the silent killer. Maybe, it was a silent message from God. With four of us, we did bring a pack mule to carry any necessary supplies plus the personal effects of the deceased vigilantes. The horses and tack of those killed had been forfeited to Rising Cross Ranch, hardly just compensation for the deadly intentions of the vigilantes. We were ever aware of our environment. Vigilance was critically important, especially in these days when the fires of fear and hatred were being stoked. The hills and trees along our route afforded plenty of opportunity for bushwhackers to ambush careless travelers.

About halfway to Bandera, I spotted what appeared to be a small Apache hunting party a quarter mile off, but we ignored each other. I wasn't looking to find out what they were hunting for. Aside from the one Apache sighting, the journey to Bandera was uneventful. If anyone had spotted us, they'd likely have thought twice about taking on such a tough-looking band.

We camped along the Medina River about an hour's ride from Bandera.

———

WE RODE SLOWLY, single file into Bandera just about the time the sun crested the eastern horizon. Frost coated the landscape, and vapors from our breathing hung in the air. I even felt a shiver run through Big Red's flanks. We rode on easy-like. Then, I felt that telltale chill that always coursed through me when danger lurked. But for the creak of our leather saddles and jingle of spurs, there was hardly a sound to be heard. It was early, but I figured some folks ought to be up and busying themselves. I led the way to Klappenbach's store. We dismounted, hitched our cayuses, and strode to the door. It was locked. I rapped on the door. Not a sound came from within. No scuffle of feet, no greetings. I shrugged. "Check out back, Shorty," I said, as I scanned the street. Where was everybody? I looked up the street to Sheriff Hoffman's jailhouse. There was a light on inside.

"No one back there, boss," reported Shorty upon his return from checking out the buildings behind the store.

The hotel a bit farther up the street from the jail was new. I reckoned it likely had some sort of restaurant. "Let's grab some grub and then visit the sheriff," I decided.

We led our horses up the street. I glanced at the jail as we passed by. There was a lantern blazing, but I could see no one.

As we approached the hotel, a young fellow passed by. "Pardon, son. Where is everybody?" I asked. I called him son, though he likely was not but a year or two younger than me.

He gave me a furtive look. "Big shootin' last night. Everybody be half scared to death."

"Anybody killed?" I had to ask the obvious question.

"No...but they still be 'round," he advised and scampered on his way.

Well, that accounted for folks laying low. I led the men up the hotel steps and opened the door. "Anybody home?" I called and stepped into the foyer. It was tastefully decorated and about as quiet as the rest of the town.

A young woman appeared. "Who you be?"

"I'm Jack O'Toole. We're here from up north with business in Bandera. Not looking for any trouble." I tried to reassure her that we were peaceful-minded. "Y'all serve breakfast here?"

She breathed a sigh of relief and pointed to a room beside the foyer. "I'm Lucy Evans. Find yourselves seats, and I'll see to your breakfast. I'll get y'all some coffee, eggs, biscuits, and ham, okay?" She skedaddled off to what was apparently the kitchen before we could respond.

We grabbed seats at a corner table with unobstructed views of the hotel front window and dining room doors. Lucy dutifully appeared with mugs and a steaming pot of coffee. "Hear tell y'all had some shooting last night?" I ventured.

"Terrible lot," she responded. She shook her head. "Doc's caring for a couple of wounded men."

"Any idea what it was about?" I asked.

"Started in the saloon. Men drinking too much. There was shouting about slaves and abolition. Then the gunfire began. Lots of shooting. Good thing nobody killed...yet," she said with a conspiratorial expression.

I shook my head. The town's mood was sitting on a knife's edge. "So, folks are hiding?"

"Sheriff arrested two, but their friends want to bust them out of jail. Sheriff Hoffman is lying low with his deputy," added Lucy.

That accounted for seeing light but no human forms inside Hoffman's jail office. Miss Evans seemed right talkative, so I reckoned to see what else I might learn. "You happen to know a fellow named Rolf Schultz?"

Lucy sniffed the air. "Oh my, the eggs be burning!" She turned and ran to the kitchen.

Shorty and Hardy savored a few sips of coffee, while Brawny eased over to the window. "All quiet, Mr. O'Toole," he said in a low voice. "There be a man with a rifle atop the buildin' beside the jail. Figure there be another on the roof of this here hotel."

Lucy returned with breakfast. The eggs were a tad browned but edible enough for hungry cowboys. "Y'all asked something afore I went to save the eggs?"

"Just wondering whether you'd heard of a fellow named Rolf Schultz?"

"Mr. Schultz! Oh my, he live upstairs. Pays on time. Dresses himself real fine." She began to paint a picture of the man allegedly responsible for nearly murdering me.

"Sounds like a gentleman," I ventured.

"Oh yes. I hear he's from New Orleans. He talks with a real sweet sound."

I recalled passing through Louisiana many years back with my pa and ma. There were folks they called Cajuns that sported accents. This left me to ponder how a man with a German last name might speak with a Cajun accent? Lucy refilled my coffee, as I took my final bites of breakfast. "Has this Mr. Schultz stirred up any trouble?"

Lucy gave me a curious look. "Not that I know of, but you can ask him yourself," she said, pointing to the dining room entrance. There stood a well-dressed man of medium proportions. He had a pointed chin accentuated by a neatly trimmed beard and mustache. Spectacles sat upon the bridge of his nose. His tailored clothes were set off with an emerald-green satin vest with gold buttons.

Upon seeing me, Schultz's eyes grew wide. "Someone asking about me," he said with an invitingly smooth Cajun accent.

I pushed back from the table and stood. "Howdy. My name's Jack O'Toole...but I think you know that." I realized that I towered over the man physically. The lingering question would be whether I towered over him thinking-wise.

Schultz shook his head. "Er…I don't think so." Even his accent failed to hide the lie.

"That's an outright lie, Mr. Schultz." I didn't figure to mince words.

His hand went to his waistband as though reaching for a gun.

"That's not a good idea," I said.

Schultz found himself staring down the barrels of three Colt revolvers. I hadn't even pulled leather.

"Let's mosey over to the jail." I dropped a gold piece on the table. "Thanks, Lucy," I added and motioned Schultz toward the front door.

"Er…boss?" murmured Brawny, motioning toward the rooftops as we approached the front door.

"I think Mr. Schultz here won't let anything happen. Will you, Rolf?" I shoved the muzzle of my now-drawn gun into the small of his back. "Keep an eye out, men."

We began what appeared to be a rather confident stroll across the street to the jail. Shorty and Hardy flanked Schultz and me while Brawny stayed on the steps of the hotel with a bead on the gunman atop the roof beside the jail. We climbed the two steps to the jail front door, and I pushed Schultz through the doorway ahead of us.

"What's this about?" challenged Sheriff Hoffman from behind a row of steel-barred cells.

"My name is Jack O'Toole, and I'm accusing this here Mr. Rolf Schultz of conspiring to murder," I said in as firm a voice as I could muster.

Hoffman emerged from behind the cells. I caught a knowing look between him and Schultz. This didn't bode well. "You got witnesses?"

"Dying man's confession, Sheriff," I said.

"Nobody to testify in a court of law?" he asked.

I shook my head. This wasn't going the way I'd envisioned.

"Just your word doesn't cut it, O'Toole." Hoffman looked from Shorty to Hardy. "Weren't you a Texas Ranger?" he asked Hardy.

Hardy nodded.

"You ought to know better than to bring someone in with no evidence," he said with a holier-than-thou tone. He turned back to me. "Ain't you that rancher they say helps slaves escape?"

"I don't help slaves...only free men," I stated firmly and truthfully. So far as I was concerned, once a slave had escaped, he was a free man. "A gang of vigilantes tried to lunch me at my ranch. A survivor said this here Rolf Schultz put them up to it. Three of them lie in their graves, and we have their personal effects to be returned to the ranches they worked for."

"Who shot those citizens?" queried Hoffman accusingly.

I looked across the street at Brawny. This was not going well at all. "A passerby looking to stop an injustice," I answered. I pulled down my shirt collar to reveal the bruises on my neck left behind by the rope. "The passerby saved my life."

I decided to change tactics. "I hear y'all had a bit of trouble last night. Might the two men stationed on the roofs looking down on your jail have anything to do with it?"

Hoffman motioned his head toward the two men occupying one of his cells. "Drunken brawl over this slave business," he informed me. But he wasn't to be dissuaded from the vigilante matter at hand. "Guess I better post a reward for the arrest of the person that murdered those three cowboys," suggested Hoffman.

"Mr. Schultz, I apologize for these ruffians. You're free to leave."

Shorty realized what was happening. "I'll get those personal effects, Mr. O'Toole." He exited ahead of Schultz, took a cautionary glance up at the rooftops, and headed toward Brawny. The man on the rooftop beside the jail stood and took aim at Shorty. A shot rang out, and the bushwhacker tumbled lifelessly to the street. Gunsmoke wafted from Brawny's revolver, and Shorty ran the last few steps to his side.

Hoffman dashed from the jail into the street with rifle in hand. The man on the hotel roof fired at near point-blank range and shot the sheriff's hat off.

Schultz emerged. "Stop!" he commanded. He'd lost that sweet Cajun voice.

The man on the hotel roof ducked down.

Shorty warned Brawny. "Get out of town. Sheriff's putting out a warrant for whoever killed the three vigilantes. Meet you where we camped."

Brawny didn't appear to have any intention of moving a muscle.

There was so much evil in the air. Lies were stacked on lies built upon fears and prejudices. It was clear that justice wasn't to be served this day.

Hoffman ducked back to the jail door and watched Schultz cross the street and enter the hotel. He then turned to me. "You get yourself back to wherever you come from, O'Toole. Don't show up back here in Bandera any time soon. I can't guarantee your safety."

Those last words were revealing. He was at his wits' end trying to keep the peace at a time when the fires of emotion over slavery were burning across Texas and the nation.

Shorty appeared in the doorway with the sack

containing the personal effects of the dead vigilantes and dropped it at Hoffman's feet. "I don't take kindly to folks who ain't truthful, Sheriff. You need to do some soul-searching." His eyes riveted on Hoffman's. "You can return these yourself. Anyone wants to know where the bodies are buried, look up along the Guadalupe River on the Rising Cross spread. Anyone makes trouble, we'll be sure to end it...peacefully, of course."

I couldn't have said it better myself. I was glad the words came from Shorty, as it wouldn't do for me to appear to threaten Hoffman. "We'll be leaving Bandera, Sheriff. Just have to stop by Klappenbach's and settle accounts." With that, I led Shorty and Hardy out the door.

Schultz, a sneering smile gracing his lips, stood at the front door of the hotel, watching our departure.

———

BEING NONE-TOO-WELCOME IN BANDERA, we were nevertheless determined to find Klappenbach. There were business loose ends to tie up, plus I was concerned as to the welfare of him and his wife Stella. He wasn't at his store or the livery. Where might he have gone? We walked our horses up the street toward Klappenbach's store.

I looked over and caught Brawny thumbing through the pages of the Bible I'd given him. He had decided to not heed Shorty's advice and head out of Bandera. I had what folks call an *ah-ha* moment. If I wasn't a fighting man and reckoned to seek sanctuary from impending violence, where might I go? Not fifty yards away was a log structure perhaps twenty by thirty feet with a sign gracing its entry: St. Stanislaus Catholic Church. Candles were burning inside, and the faint sound of voices could be heard.

I hadn't been inside a church since my days growing up back in Pennsylvania. My only religious teachings were from my pa and ma. My Irish Catholic heritage had long gone. I expect I was what folks called a Protestant. Still, I'd never given thought to labeling my faith. I had a feeling that Klappenbach and his wife would be inside, along with a few other citizens of Bandera. I doffed my hat, scratched my head, and headed for the church.

"Where you headed, boss?" asked Shorty, even though my intentions were obvious.

"Hang here with the horses, Shorty."

I pushed the church door open. The sanctuary was crowded with roughly twenty worried-looking citizens. The light was dim, and the smells of candle wax and an over-burdened privy combined with all manner of competing odors. I figured these folks had holed up here for better than a day. I caught Klappenbach's eye and motioned him to me.

Klappenbach squeezed his way through the crowded church and extended a hand. "Good to see you, Jack. But it's a dangerous time to come to Bandera."

I shook his hand. "I won't be staying long, August." Here was my partner in two trail drives, a solid businessman whom I admired, and he was cowering before some hombres stirring up the town. "Just wanted to settle up from the trail drive." I handed him a sack with a couple of hundred dollars in gold coins.

"Heard you got roughed up by some vigilance committee. You okay?"

"Word gets around," I said with a nod.

"Have you talked with Sheriff Hoffman? Hear tell he's looking for the vigilante killer."

"The world's a tad upside down these days, August. The sheriff should be hunting down the vigilantes, not chasing the man who saved my life." About now, I found myself regretting turning over the personal effects of the three dead vigilantes to the lawman. I truly wanted to confront the owners of the ranches from where those men came. It was too late now...or was it?

Klappenbach's eyes riveted in on me. "Don't even think it, Jack." He'd read my mind.

"What are you doing in here with the trouble brewing outside?" I figured to challenge my friend a bit.

"Stella dragged me here," he confessed. He swept back his coat to reveal a Colt revolver in his waistband, as though assuring me he was no coward.

I smiled. "I understand, my friend. It's looking like the trouble has blown over for now. One bushwhacker is dead, and that Schultz fellow silenced the other."

"Danged troublemaker that one," observed Klappenbach.

"One of the vigilante's dying words were that Schultz stirred them into the hateful frenzy that led them to try to lunch me. Sheriff Hoffman says the man's dying words won't stand in a courtroom, so he won't arrest Schultz."

Klappenbach shook his head ruefully. "Hoffman is Schultz's man, Jack."

"Reckoned as such," I responded. "I figure to have Shorty head up the next drive. My coming down here would only stir up trouble."

"Wise move," agreed Klappenbach.

"Folks up in Kerrville seem friendlier," I noted.

"It's those Germans. Hear tell they don't cotton to slavery. I expect it could spell trouble afore long."

"There's big struggles brewing, August. I can sense it. That raid on the Harpers Ferry arsenal was just the beginning. Been all that bleeding up in Kansas the past few years, too. It seems there's nothing peaceful about the slavery question."

Klappenbach nodded. "I've tried to stay clear. It sure isn't good for business or health."

"I figure all of Texas is going to catch fire, August." I scratched my chin. "Actually, I reckon the whole country might. I don't know that there's any escape. Evil men fan the flames and folks up against each other. Hard to figure why except that they seek power and control."

"You're wise beyond your years, Jack O'Toole," observed Klappenbach.

"Well, I must go, August." I scanned the sanctuary. The folks were still frightened. "*Buena suerte*, my friend." We shook hands, and I headed from the church.

I stood at the doorway a moment and made a quick scan of the area to be sure there were no more bush-whackers lurking. "Let's go, Shorty," I said. I paused. Over in the corral beside the livery stood a black stallion. There was something familiar about it, but I couldn't quite put my finger on whatever it was. As I turned away, the stallion's single white forelock caught my eye. I felt as though I'd seen the cayuse before, but...

We mounted up with me in the lead, and Shorty, Hardy, and Brawny following. We were anxious to get back to Rising Cross Ranch, as Christmas was but a couple of days off. As we passed the hotel, Rolf Schultz stood at the front door. His expressionless face sent a chill up my spine. This was one very dangerous man. I reckoned him to be the Devil, Lucifer, Satan, Mephistopheles, and the Antichrist incarnate. There'd surely be future trouble yet to be faced with this man. We rode on silently. There seemed no point in dealing with Schultz for now.

———

WE RODE three or four miles in silence. The cloudless sky seemed to demand reverent silence.

It wasn't until our first crossing of the meandering route of the Medina River that Hardy broke the ice. "Schultz is trouble, boss. He's bankrolled by money from back east."

"You know him?" I asked tentatively.

"Heard of him," answered Hardy. "Texas Rangers under Captain Benton nearly killed him a year or so back. He was involved in some slave selling deal. He escaped. If the Rangers hadn't been defunded, they might have caught him." Hardy shook his head resignedly. "He does have a weakness, as I understand it."

I pulled up. "What's that?"

"You saw some of it in Bandera, boss. He's arrogant."

I knew from experience that arrogance breeds carelessness. "Good to know, Hardy. Thanks." I looked back at Shorty and Brawny. "You heard that. Any trouble comes, it'll likely be Schultz's doing."

As we rode on, I hoped that Spirit Talker and Prairie Flower would be at the ranch for a Christmas visit. I sure missed my Comanche brother.

THREE
CHRISTMAS

THE SMOKE PIROUETTING skyward from the ranch house was a welcome sight on the horizon ahead of us. The temperature had plummeted during the night, so we were bundled up as best we could against the cold. There was a heaviness in the air that hinted of snow, a rarity in this part of Texas.

Tough as the frontier has made me, I found myself anxious to hold Blue Flower in my arms and cuddle with my children. The warm hearth and the closeness of family and friends would be most welcome, especially after the events in Bandera. I figured it would be ever-less-safe for me to do business in the cowboy town, given the rumors swirling around concerning my feelings over slavery. Rolf Schultz would surely keep those rumors stirred up. I'd begun to think that we might be better off dealing with the folks in Kerrville for our supplies.

As we drew closer to the ranch house, I saw Spirit Talker's teepee erected beside the barn. My heart raced at the prospect of a few days of my Comanche friend's companionship. Even Zeb got excited and raced ahead. "Looks like Mukwooru is here," I said to no one in particular.

Brawny spotted the teepee. "That's yer Comanche friend, ain't it?"

"Yes. We've pulled each other out of a few scrapes," I replied.

"He ever do any scalpin'?" asked the former slave catcher.

I laughed and nudged Big Red to a faster pace. "You'll have to ask him."

"Is it true what folks say about Comanche torture?" called out Brawny, as I rode ahead.

"Worse," I shouted back, intent on closing the distance to home.

———

WE PULLED up in a cloud of frozen dust with me several horse lengths ahead. Blue Flower heard Zeb's approach and opened the front door just as I dismounted. Oh my, but she was a beautiful sight.

She ran into my arms. "Pohya Isa home!" she declared, as she sought to fuse herself with my chest. "*Kamakuna, kamakuna.*" The Comanche words for loved one poured from her lips. Lips? She kissed me long and passionately. Shorty and the others turned away out of embarrassment.

"Pohya Isa!" came a voice from behind me.

Blue Flower eased her embrace enough for me to look over my shoulder and greet Spirit Talker and Prairie Flower. "*Pabi!* Welcome, brother," I replied to his greeting. "*Ana o'a hi'it.*" I invited them to come and eat, though in looking into Blue Flower's eyes, food was not on my menu. But friends came first. We were hungry.

"Doggone, boss, talk English," urged Hardy.

My habit of conversing with Spirit Talker and the rest of my Comanche family with a mix of English and Comanche, came naturally to me. It seemed a sign of mutual respect. "Guess I'll have to teach you the language, Hardy. Maybe teach Shorty here some Lakota while we're at it." I laughed at the realization that the prospects for survival on the frontier were enhanced if we could communicate with the tribes. It occurred to me that we were now standing around in the cold, surrounded by the white vapors from our breath. "Let's all go inside," I urged.

With an arm around Blue Flower, I led the way inside. Four little arms embraced my legs, as I walked through the threshold. George and Isa were walking now and gurgling a mix of simple English and Comanche words. I looked around and saw baby Peter asleep in his cradleboard.

Blue Flower gave my hand a loving squeeze and headed to the stove to heat up some coffee. Prairie Flower followed, and I smiled as they animatedly discussed what to feed us.

Perez poked his head in. "*Amigos*, take care of your horses and come eat at the bunkhouse."

Shorty caught on right quickly. It was time to let the family get reacquainted. "I'll take care of Big Red, boss," he said with a wink as he headed out the door.

Blue Flower set four cups on the table and filled them with steaming-hot coffee. She turned back to the stove to fix some ham and eggs. "How Bandera?" she asked over her shoulder.

I sighed. "Not what we expected. I was glad to have Shorty, Hardy, and Brawny along."

"Brawny Jones?" asked Spirit Talker. "The slave catcher?"

"He's turned to God." I paused. "He saved my life from what we call vigilantes, folks that take their version of the law into their own hands. I was nearly hung." I lowered my shirt collar and revealed the still-vivid black and blue welts from the noose.

Spirit Talker took a long sip of hot coffee. "God *natsuitu* in you, Jack. *Natsuitu sunipu.* He look over you. Always sends help."

He was right. My medicine, my *sunipu,* was strong owing to my faith in God. Oh, I had help from family and friends, but those who followed me seemed to be drawn to me by some force beyond my reckoning. Perhaps, it was my honesty and sense of fair play. Could it be my belief in redemption and striving for just outcomes? I had learned to never hold back my sense of truth, of what was right. Even what was most loved might have to be sacrificed to a higher outcome as assured by my God. It was like Abraham offering to sacrifice his son Isaac. I reached down and scratched Zeb's mane. "I am Walk With Wolves," I offered as a verbal punctuation to my thoughts. I thought on the vigilantes and how they had bought into Schultz's lies about me. It seemed that the lies about slavery were like a poison spreading across the nation. People the likes of Schultz found ways to gain power through depending on people believing the lies. Journalists like Gordon Small used the power of the printed word to spread news with whatever perspectives they felt would sell newspapers. Even my erstwhile friend Rip Ford owned a newspaper that was slanted in support of the economic interests of slaveholders in Texas.

Blue Flower brought a platter filled with eggs, ham slices, and buttered biscuits to the table and sat beside me. She placed her hand on the one I was using to scratch Zeb. "Jack *kamacuna* to *numunuu*."

She was right I reckoned, as I followed Blue Flower, Spirit Talker, and Prairie Flower in heaping my plate with God's bounty. I was blessed by being loved by many people.

Spirit Talker nodded at Blue Flower's succinct description of why folks ascribed their loyalty to me. "Buffalo Hump tell me to listen to the wind, for it talks, to listen to the silence, as it speaks, but above all to listen to your heart. Your heart knows."

My Comanche brother had spoken with the wisdom learned from his father, the powerful and well-respected Penateka Comanche chief. I nodded. "We face great danger here. If we stay, we must be ever mindful of more vigilantes or worse. There's a man in Bandera named Rolf Schultz who tells lies about me to stir people to hate me. Yet to leave seems the coward's way out."

"What you do here at Rising Cross in winter?" asked Spirit Talker.

It was an interesting question. "We make sure the livestock survives the winter."

He nodded. "Come spend winter with Penateka."

I felt Blue Flower squeeze my hand. My free hand wrapped around the coffee mug, and I stared thoughtfully into the dark brew. "Will and Kate are here. Shorty runs the operation," I said, thinking out loud. I liked the idea that Spirit Talker's village was far enough from the growing threat looming nearby. I gazed into Blue Flower's eyes. Her beautiful, deep-brown eyes had a way of persuading me of things with nary a word spoken. "Sounds good," I finally blurted.

Spirit Talker offered a broad grin. He still bore the scars from the mountain lion attack years back, yet they brought a rough but handsome sort of character to his facial expression.

Blue Flower stood and pranced to the cabinet beside the stove. "We celebrate," she said over her shoulder, as she drew out a platter of bear sign which she promptly brought to the table.

"We'll go after Christmas," I said decisively. It was as though a great load had been lifted from my shoulders. I felt relieved. Should I have been? The poison of the slavery issue seemed destined to continue its spread. Could it be resolved in a rational manner by honest men? I feared that the antidote might yet be some terrible conflict. Men like Schultz stirred up the hate and discontent that fueled the flames of discord.

A knock at the door silenced us. If it was one of the men, they'd knock and barge on in. I arose and walked to the door with my hand resting on the butt of the Colt revolver in my holster. Shorty and the others were down at the bunkhouse. I was surprised that they hadn't been alerted to the arrival of a guest. Even Zeb hadn't stirred. "Who goes?" I asked.

"Sheriff," came the response.

I opened the door to find Sheriff Hoffman standing before me. He stood shivering in a wet duster. A chill rain had begun, and he hadn't been quite prepared for it. "Come on in, Sheriff."

He took a step inside but paused at seeing a Comanche warrior and two women. "You okay?" he asked.

Blue Flower had already moved to pour a cup of coffee which she held out to him.

Hoffman accepted it tentatively.

"Sheriff, this is my wife, Blue Flower, and these are my dear friends, Spirit Talker and Prairie Flower." With that, my twins appeared and wrapped themselves around my legs.

"Er...quite a family, Mr. O'Toole." He hesitated, then turned to Blue Flower. "Thank you, ma'am."

"Have a seat and warm your bones, Sheriff," I urged. "What brings you to Rising Cross? Seems like we were in your office just a couple of days back."

Hoffman glanced around furtively. There was no doubt that he held no love for the Red man, but he'd come on a mission. "Just felt it fair to warn you," he managed to spew out in a guarded voice. "I dropped some of those personal effects at the Waterson place. The owner and his hands were none too pleased. I heard chatter about revenge." He paused. All eyes were on him. "I'd watch your back."

"Thanks kindly for the warning, Sheriff." I sat opposite him. "You're welcome to stay until the rain lets up."

Hoffman seemed both agitated and relieved. Then he noticed Zeb. Now, he found himself in the company of Comanche and a wolf. He gave me a quizzical look.

Spirit Talker laughed. "Jack save me from mountain lion. We friends. Blue Flower my sister. This my wife Topsannah. I am son of Buffalo Hump, chief of Penateka Comanche."

I think Hoffman was as much taken aback by the information as by an Indian speaking the English language.

"He's got it about right, Sheriff," I added with a smile.

Hoffman nodded and looked questioningly at Zeb.

Now, it was my turn. "Zeb is my loyal protector. His name means gift from God. I saved the life of his mate, and he's been with me ever since. He's tame." I paused, "unless threatened."

"How'd you get here?" pressed Hoffman.

"Folks homesteaded. They were killed in a Comanche attack along with one of my brothers and a sister. I survived. With Spirit Talker's help, I rescued a brother and sister that were kidnapped. We have a strong bond."

Hoffman shook his head thoughtfully, as he sought to absorb my story. The frontier was filled with stories of the sort of events and outcomes I'd just described, but it was not so common to actually meet someone who'd lived the adventure I'd described. Hoffman gave me a hard gaze. "I been around Indians a bit, Mr. O'Toole. Some can be peaceful like your family." He looked off, and it was clear that he had some profound observation to add—likely one that colored his view of the Red man. "I knew White men that entered an Indian village and were welcomed and fed. When they departed, the same Indians that fed them hunted them down to kill and take scalps. There be no mercy or the like." He let that sink in. "If you put up a good fight against an Indian, they respect you and likely let you live. Otherwise, they be savages. You and I know that many folks under attack save a bullet for themselves rather than fall into the clutches of the hostiles and be tortured to death."

I nodded. Hoffman was right about how some folks ended their lives rather than be captured. Many tribes were exceptionally evil, when it came to torturing victims. My mind's eye held an indelible picture of my own ma's end at the hands of the Comanche. "I appreciate what you say, Sheriff. I believe that there are many misunderstandings among the races, whether White, Red, Black, or Brown. Call it a clash of cultures, if you will. Differences in language and culture pose considerable challenges to understanding and any resulting peace." I paused to reflect a moment. "But you're here about my views as to enslaved Blacks. By my observation, Sheriff, nobody's ever had the inclination to understand the culture of the Blacks—just as they don't for the Indians or Mexicans. Folks tend to be self-serving, thinking only of themselves."

Hoffman took a long sip of coffee.

I felt as though I was achieving a middle ground of sorts with the sheriff. I wasn't sure he liked the possibility of having his ingrained set of beliefs changed. It was unlikely that I'd dissuade him from his prejudices, but I held hope that he would not be an enemy. "You ever been up to the North Platte country, Sheriff?"

He shook his head.

"It's beautiful. Majestic mountains, fast-flowing rivers, crystal-clear skies," I waxed eloquently. "And freezing cold, snow-filled winters," I added with a laugh.

"You against slavery, Mr. O'Toole?" Hoffman steered me back to the root of his purpose here this day.

I sighed resignedly. "I believe it's immoral. Am I against it? Yes."

Hoffman's eyes widened. "That translates to plenty of trouble for you, Mr. O'Toole."

"You read the Bible, Sheriff?"

He nodded.

"Do you believe holding another human in bondage is right? Is it moral?" I kept my voice easy-like. I didn't want to come off as threatening.

"There ain't no law against it," he responded defensively.

"There's God's law," I continued. "Remember that God freed the enslaved Hebrews from Egypt? And Christ preaches that man is only enslaved to God."

Hoffman folded his arms across his chest. "Blacks only good as slaves," he countered.

I took another tack. "My Pa taught me that our Declaration of Independence says we are endowed by our Creator with certain inalienable rights that among these are life, liberty, and the pursuit of happiness. It doesn't say only White men have liberty."

Hoffman squirmed, then sat upright and wrapped his hands around the coffee mug. "You're pushing me, O'Toole," he said testily.

There was no respectful *mister* in front of my name. Just then, there was a knock at the door. "Who goes?" I called out, appreciating the interruption.

"Hey, boss. It's me, Brawny."

"Come on in."

"Thought you could use more firewood." The door swept open, and Brawny stepped in and deposited an armload of split wood beside the fireplace. "Rain's stopped for now," he observed. He nodded to the sheriff and headed for the door.

"Thanks, Brawny," I said as he closed the door behind him. I turned to Hoffman. "Do you know who that man is?" I asked.

Hoffman shook his head.

"That's Brawny Jones. He's caught dozens of escaped slaves for the bounties. You think he'd be hanging around here if he had a problem with my views on slavery?"

Again, the sheriff shook his head. "I expect not," he finally said.

Spirit Talker poured a bit of fuel on the conversational

flames. "Comanche make slaves of people taken in battle. Sometimes set free." He shrugged. "Redskins...Whites... Blacks... Browns all have evil people among them. Slavery not good. Men free as wind."

Hoffman shifted uncomfortably.

Zeb's low growl told me that he sensed an evil emanating from the sheriff.

"Keep that beast away," demanded Hoffman. The sheriff had had enough. He didn't much appreciate the impact we were having on him as concerned his point of view about slavery. He stood and donned his still soaking-wet slicker. "I just come out here to warn y'all. Rain or no, I'm heading back to Bandera."

I stood and offered a handshake.

Hoffman ignored my hand. "Thanks for the coffee," he snarled and bolted out the door.

I flinched as the door slammed behind the sheriff. I turned to Spirit Talker. "Guess spending a few weeks with our *numunuu* is a good idea," I offered with a smile. By calling the Comanche *our* people, I was acknowledging them being far more accepting of my beliefs than my own race.

———

EARLY CHRISTMAS MORNING might best have been described as a sort of organized chaos. The women, with Perez's help, were busy preparing a feast worthy of the day while children roamed about underfoot and babies sought seemingly endless feeding. I did my best to dress up for the occasion, though there were plenty of chores to be tended to despite the holy day. It was a tad humbling. Mucking stalls, for example, was a reminder of Christ's simple beginnings lying in a lowly manger surrounded by livestock. I sat for a few moments sipping coffee and watching Blue Flower admiringly as she directed the preparation of the Christmas dinner. Even the experienced trail cook, Perez, yielded to her orders.

Finally, and having been fully overwhelmed by the delicious aromas being created, I donned my wolfskin vest and headed for the barn. Zeb followed dutifully. I arrived to greet Buck with shovel in hand. He shoved a second shovel at me, and I pitched in. Shorty and Hardy arrived from having checked the northernmost pastures. Will and Brawny rode in soon thereafter from the south range. They men reported that all was well among cattle and horses. The only casualty had been an aged horse that fell victim to a pair of mountain lions. That was a sad outcome, as every life was precious. It served as a reminder that the frontier was about the survival of the fittest. I was pleased that the men traveled in pairs for their own safety—if there was such a thing these days.

Upon completing the chores around the barn, we all meandered to the bunkhouse to await the call for Christmas dinner. Spirit Talker and Isaac joined us. There were enough of us to potentially yield many hours of tall tales. As it was, I figured we'd have at least an hour to regale each other with exaggerated stories of our adventures during the past year. I took the opportunity to share my conversation with Sheriff Hoffman. All agreed that my leaving the ranch and spending a couple of months with the Penateka Comanche made sense. We all hoped it would allow the emotionally heated contentions in the region to cool a bit.

We'd managed to make ourselves reasonably presentable for a feast honoring Christ's birth. I was already beginning to think on how I'd soon be wearing buckskins and joining Spirit Talker on hunts with bow and arrow. The dinner bell broke my erstwhile meditations on the future. We—eight ravishingly hungry men—made a beeline for the door. The bunkhouse wall actually shook as we hit the doorway. Shorty had come to an abrupt halt, and we all plowed into his back.

"I'm hit," Shorty called out. An arrow protruded from his shoulder.

I retreated upon hearing the distinctive thud of arrows into the doorjamb. One flew past my ear. We dove for whatever weapons we could grab and quickly positioned ourselves at the windows. About a dozen Kiowa had decided to have their own celebration. We poured lead into them as fast as we could. At least three savages had fallen from their ponies, when Blue Flower—having heard the shooting and war whoops—emerged from our house with my Sharps rifle in hand. I saw the apparent leader of the hostiles turn toward her. He was a menacing figure on an appaloosa pony decorated with warpaint. He was shielded from my line of sight momentarily, though I could see him raise his lance. An expression of horror surely crossed my face at the possibility of the love of my life being attacked by the savage. Then... well...then, I heard the booming report of the Sharps. It was as though a cannon had been fired. I saw the Kiowa leader fly from his pony, dead before his body hit the ground. The remaining Kiowa warriors, having seen their leader blown from this world, went into near-instant retreat.

We cautiously emerged from the bunkhouse. Blue Flower stood in a haze of gun smoke. She caught my eyes, smiled, and went back inside the cabin as though nothing had happened. Four dead Kiowa littered the space between my house and the bunkhouse. Perez stepped from the house and rang the dinner bell. The bodies would wait. We headed inside to tend to Shorty's wound and to sit down to enjoy Christmas dinner. As I stepped through the doorway, Blue Flower was sitting at the table, shaking like a leaf. The image of killing the hostile must have finally overwhelmed her senses. I rushed over and took her in my arms, drying her tears with my bandanna.

"Jack smell like gun smoke," she finally said.

I'll bet I did. With her nerves settled, she kissed me lightly and gave me a loving look before joining Prairie Flower, Kate, and Sarah in serving up our feast. In mere moments, what normally would have been the horror of having been attacked by hostile savages was pretty much forgotten.

Perez busied himself tending to Shorty's wound, which turned out to not be serious. My ranch foreman was able to join in our Christmas dinner right quickly, as appetite triumphed over any pain.

We had a lot to be thankful for this Christmas, and I did my best to recall everything as part of my dinner blessing. How many Christmas dinner celebrations begin with an Indian attack? This one would not be soon forgotten. It was a vivid reminder of how vulnerable we were. Had the Kiowa caught us between the bunkhouse and our dinner, the outcome might have been plenty different. "Thank you, Lord and amen," I said, punctuating the blessing.

FOUR
LIFE WITH THE COMANCHE

THE PEDERNALES RIVER ran pretty-strong this time of year. The Penateka Comanche respected it, though I wasn't so sure the folks far downstream in Fredericksburg reciprocated. I found accommodating the life in a Comanche village easier than I'd expected. The day-to-day life easily led me to wondering how these peaceful *numunuu* could be the ever-menacing denizens of the Comancheria, the most fearsome warriors to ride the frontier. I observed the warriors instructing the young boys in the skills they would need to hunt and fight. It was the fight part that concerned me, as their use of knife, lance, war club, and bow and arrows—while sounding fearsome—paled in comparison to the weapons used by Whites. Repeating rifles and revolvers were far superior to what the Comanche could bring to a fight. Couple this with Whites having vastly superior numbers of fighters that were constantly replenished, and the Comanche days were numbered.

Blue Flower easily fell into the routines she'd grown up with as the daughter of a chief, and our twins George and Isa were as happy as I'd ever seen them. Gathering as a family in the confines of our own teepee did seem to bring us closer together, though I must admit to cherishing the opportunities to be out hunting game.

Big Red was not a big fan of being kept with the hundreds of Comanche ponies. He stood a couple of hands taller than most of them and missed his familiar brood back at Rising Cross. I wound up staking him close by with Blue Flower's mare.

The encampment seemed to accommodate Zeb's presence. The Comanche revered the wolf for its qualities of loyalty, strength, leadership, cunning, and bravery, so Zeb fit well into their cultural beliefs. That having been said, only me, Spirit Talker, and our immediate families were allowed within Zeb's chosen circle. A quick snarl or warning growl sufficed to keep all others at bay. How he found time to lead his own pack was a wonder to me. He would disappear for long periods of up to a week but invariably return to me.

Any concerns I had about Rising Cross Ranch were much abated by Buffalo Hump's scouting parties that kept us informed as to goings on. While the still-influential chief was growing old and his days were numbered, he nevertheless thoroughly enjoyed our extended visit.

Many an evening, we sat around Buffalo Hump's fire discussing the goings on in the world that was increasingly overrun by the White man. Like me, he lamented the prejudices that were leading to violence. We especially talked about the plight of the Blacks, but dared not give short shrift to the intolerance of Mexicans and Indians. That *numunuu* should be defined solely by the color of their skin was seen as an abomination. We all worried that a dire future of much bloodshed awaited us all.

Living among the Comanche served as a temporary

escape from the threats lingering back home. The day-to-day chores of an Indian village consumed most waking hours. There were horses to tend, weapons to fashion, knives to sharpen, and the occasional hunt. There were no war parties formed. With winter upon us, there seemed no inclination to go off and fight. Importantly, no one was threatening the village.

———

ON A CRISP EARLY MARCH MORNING, Spirit Talker, three warriors, and I embarked on a hunt. Venison was on our minds, though we wouldn't be overly fussy about any mammal bearing edible meat. The hibernation season was just about at an end, so we'd be especially alert for hungry sows with newborn cubs. Spirit Talker and I had dealt with grizzlies in the past, so we were well aware of what we would be dealing with should such an encounter occur. There were other predators on the hunt besides bears. We'd had our past run-in with mountain lions, bobcats could be nasty, and there were wolves and coyotes to contend with. Having Zeb along and knowing that his pack was close by was reassuring.

Furry predators were plentiful, and in truth, the least of our worries. The predations of ill-intentioned humans were of greater concern. Lawbreakers and other roguish characters were an ever-increasing threat to the rough-edged tranquility of the frontier. Cold weather did tend to discourage lawbreakers from making trouble. As I figured it, it was more likely that a bunch of drunks in a warm saloon were better candidates for mayhem.

As pure happenstance would have it, I decided to take my trusty Sharps rifle along on this hunt. If we happened on a buffalo, the beast could be dispatched rather swiftly by virtue of its stopping power. The same could be said for just about any living creature struck by a slug from the Sharps. I was of a sporting mind, though, and reckoned to mostly rely on my very own bow and arrows. I'd worked doggedly to fashion arrows that would fly straight and true.

There was no snow, though the grasses were still a tad frozen and, despite our soft-soled moccasins, tended to crunch underfoot when we chose to walk. We would be hard-pressed to sneak up on anything undetected. Of course, our horses pretty much eliminated any hope of stealth, as they breathed heavily and occasionally nickered and snorted. Big Red was the only shod cayuse, but all the horses made greater than desirable noise on the hard ground. Had we been a war party, stealth would have been critically important, and the Comanche would have strapped leather booties on the hooves of their ponies.

My possibles bag was slung over my shoulder, affording easy access to the jerky and pemmican Blue Flower had stuffed inside. She sure made a great pemmican.

We rode silently along the south bank of the river, finding occasional deer sign. I wouldn't say we were recklessly careless, as that wasn't the Indian way, however, we were not so cautious as we should have been. We were keeping our eyes peeled for evidence of prey. Ironically, that intense sort of concentration often resulted in missing the obvious.

I happened to glance up at the crystalline clouds gracing the azure sky. Buzzards! I urged Big Red forward alongside Spirit Talker. "Mukwooru, look," I said, pointing to the sky ahead.

Our hunting party pulled up.

"Let's see what they've found," I suggested. I figured that worst case we'd happen upon a dead deer being devoured by coyotes while the birds floated patiently aloft on air currents while waiting for their leavings. I led the way, following a dry creek bed through dense stands of live oak and mountain laurel. We necessarily traveled single file.

Upon finally reaching the spot directly below the buzzards, I dismounted and led Big Red up out of the creek bed. I cautiously looked around, remounted, and led our party perhaps another fifty feet through a stand of live oak. Upon emerging from the trees, my jaw dropped. Three White men were staked out, half naked and half alive. They'd been cut badly, partially scalped, and would surely bleed out soon enough. I quickly chased off a couple of none-too-happy coyotes that had been getting up the courage to finish off the men. As I began to dismount, Spirit Talker grabbed my arm and pulled me up short.

"Wait," he said. He scanned the area with special attention to the frozen earth and an arrow protruding from the ribs of one of the victims. Whomever had done this had left little or no trace. "Steal *tosa puuka*. Maybe *taatsukwiti* Apache." He held up nine fingers to me, though I already knew enough Comanche to have understood him. The three Comanche with us didn't understand English, so Spirit Talker threw in Comanche words for their benefit. A party of nine Apache had attacked the men, tortured them, stolen their horses, and left them to die a slow death from blood loss and exposure.

While our three Comanche companions remained mounted and alert for trouble, Spirit Talker and I slipped from our horses and began cutting the bindings of the three victims. There was little we could do immediately for their wounds, so we wrapped the men in blankets and gave them water. They were already terribly weak from blood loss. Despite the possibility that the Apache were still nearby, I went to work building a fire to warm the three.

One of the men groggily opened his fear-filled eyes. At the sight of Spirit Talker and the rest of our hunting party, he passed out.

We began to whip up the Comanche healing poultices that we carried by necessity out here on the frontier. We applied them to the wounds of the three victims, though treatment seemed hopeless given their head wounds from the scalping and other deep wounds. There seemed little hope for their survival.

From what I could gather from limited evidence derived from my own quick scan of the area, they likely were hunters making camp when attacked.

Spirit Talker and one of our fellow Comanche hunters began scouting the area around the scene. It would be important to know which direction the Apache had headed with their trophies.

We were better than a two-day ride from Fredericksburg, so it would be a struggle for these badly wounded men to travel there even if they were up to it. Neither were we ready to give up our own horses, which were extremely valuable out here on the harsh hills and prairies of Central Texas. What to do? I continued to tend to the men as best I could, but the situation for them was ever more dire. The fire and blankets were warming them, but many of their wounds were grievous. I glanced up to the sky and noted that the buzzards had disappeared—for now.

"Find anything?" I asked Spirit Talker as he returned from scouting the area.

"*Tosa peeka* Apache," he responded. He held weapons taken from a dead Apache that had apparently been killed by the White men.

White Buffalo, one of our Comanche hunters, rode in behind Spirit Talker, leading a bloodied but unwounded Apache pony. What a wonderful find! We might yet give at least one of the wounded men transportation—if one could travel at all.

I turned back to the three wounded Whites struggling for life. I heard a groan from the man with the arrow wound and kneeled at his side. We'd removed the arrow, but it had apparently hit a vital organ. He was bleeding inside. Combined with the torture inflicted by the Apache savages and the chill air, he finally breathed his last. Sadly, the ground was too frozen and rocky to bury him. We'd have to place his body on a scaffold like many tribes did. Only two of the White men now lived. I hoped they would revive, as I dearly wanted to hear their story. I turned to Spirit Talker. "How far away are Apache?"

He shrugged. They might have been a hunting party that was distracted by the opportunity to attack White men, though nine warriors were a good-sized band for hunting. If they were roaming about looking for trouble, they might still be close. They surely must have known that they were treading upon Penateka Comanche territory. "If Apache see us, they no attack. Fear Comanche." He said the last words with a confident smile. "Fear Pohya Isa," he added.

I doubted the Apache had ever heard of Walks With Wolves, but I didn't mind the implied accolade from my Comanche brother.

"Help me," groaned one of the wounded men.

I went to his side. There, I was dressed in full buckskins. But for my blue eyes and blond hair sticking out from beneath my hat, I likely looked like a Comanche savage to the poor soul. "My name is Jack O'Toole. What happened here?"

He blinked as he strove to bring his sight into focus.

I put the bota bag to his lips. He nearly choked on the water. "Easy. Don't drink it all at once," I cautioned.

"Wh...Who?" he managed to ask in his weakened condition. His half-opened eyes scanned the area and came to rest on our fierce-looking band of Comanche warriors.

"We are friends." I tried to be reassuring to him. "Found y'all in quite a fix. How'd you get tangled with Apache?"

The man was obviously in considerable pain. "Sam... he hate Injuns." He tried to take a deep breath. "Sam... he shot one. Then...then, all hell broke loose." He coughed and dry-heaved. "My name is..." He passed out.

He hadn't said much. It seemed as though the White men had initiated the fight, brief as it apparently was. That wasn't unusual. Most conflicts on the frontier were brief, as Indians were generally disinclined to conduct lengthy sieges. The Apache had surely been pleased to run off with the horses, guns, and clothing taken from the three Whites.

Spirit Talker walked over. He'd been helping build a scaffold for the dead White man and another one for the Apache. Both were out of respect for the dead. "*Tosa* speak?" he asked.

"Seems the *tosas* felt threatened. The dead one shot and killed one of the Apache. He hated Red men." I shook my head. There it was. Prejudice once again had reared its ugly head.

"*Kaahaniitu peeka*," lamented Spirit Talker. Indeed, hate kills. "We help *tosas*?" He knew the answer. Had this incident occurred before I'd saved his life, Spirit Talker would have taken three scalps—if they had any to be taken.

I agreed that it seemed unjust to help the Whites who had started the fight. Then again, they'd been sorely punished for their transgressions. "God would have us help them," I counseled. "He has punished them," I added. "We must now show mercy." I could see that Spirit Talker wasn't happy with the idea, but was trying to understand.

He pondered my response. On the one hand, the men had killed an Apache, and the Apache were sworn enemies of the Comanche. On the other hand, the men had killed out of their hatred for Indians in general. It was a bit of a dilemma for him, but he strove to trust in his faith in God.

I looked over at the man who had yet to come to.

Spirit Talker followed my gaze and looked intensely at the wounded man. "Dead," he declared.

The man lay still, and his face was exceptionally pale. I walked over and confirmed Spirit Talker's judgment. Now, only one of the Whites remained, and he was barely clinging to life. "Better build another one of them," I said, pointing to the burial scaffold.

"We hunt soon," said Spirit Talker, unequivocally stating the obvious.

I was torn. We were committed to bringing meat in for our families as well as for the village. This situation had certainly put a hitch in our plans. As if on cue, I heard a gurgle. I'd heard what they call death rattles before. The third *tosa* took a final breath and died. It left me wondering what I might have done to save him? He hadn't been up to traveling, especially on horseback. Even a travois would have killed him. Could I...would

I...have abandoned him to die? I'd never know. I found myself grateful to be relieved of the burden while feeling pangs of guilt over a might-have-been.

Spirit Talker placed his hand on my shoulder. "If *tosa* live, take to Penateka *numunuu*." Bless his soul, he was trying to relieve me of the guilt that he sensed I was feeling.

I smiled. "We hunt," I announced. I went about rooting through the men's pockets for any identification. I found very little. One had been named Sam Jones and another John Jackson, but the third would remain nameless. I reckoned I'd drop their effects off in Fredericksburg next time I was in the town.

The White men and lone Apache would be left wrapped in blankets on the scaffolds. They'd likely be feasted upon by carrion, be they buzzards or coyote. In retrospect, them being on scaffolds was not likely an improvement over being staked out on the frozen ground. The best that might be said was that someone cared enough to have tried to help them.

If there was an upside to this experience it was that we'd become aware of hostile Apache in the area. I wondered whether Rip Ford's activities in South Texas against Juan Cortina might have stirred the Apache to range further northward than usual.

FINDING the victims of the Apache had certainly been eye-opening. Our hunting party was now more alert for danger. There was no telling where the Apache might be. We hadn't traveled more than an hour from the attack scene when a herd of deer came into view. We dismounted and grabbed our bows and quivers of arrows.

We each chose a target. Killing just one might have spooked the herd, so the plan was to bring down as many as possible with our first assault. Amazingly, the plan worked, and we were soon dressing our kills and tying them on the pony we'd brought along for that purpose. The cayuse was a tad skittish at first, but quickly accommodated the deer.

We were reveling in our good fortune and wending our way along a dry creek bed when we found ourselves confronted by a nasty sight. Standing before us was a wild boar and two sows. These are ugly critters. They usually weighed in at a couple of hundred pounds, and this boar was at least that big. They weren't to be trifled with. They had few natural enemies, the wolf being one of them. That likely accounted for a ferocious snarl from Zeb that caught the boar's attention.

Spirit Talker wasted no time. He nocked an arrow, and with unerring aim, loosed the shaft deep into the boar's heart. The beast grunted and dropped to his knees before rolling over on his side and breathing his last. The sows snorted, glared at us and Zeb, and took off. We heard Zeb's pack in hot pursuit.

"Great shot!" I declared to Spirit Talker. As I began to dismount to investigate our prey, we heard a great growl behind us. The pony carrying our deer reared and neighed loudly, as a hungry, snarling salivating grizzly approached it. Angry red eyes bore in on the deer.

Spirit Talker and I had fought off bears before. Of all the denizens of the frontier, an angry or even hungry bear posed a challenge to any human's life and limb. I calmly slipped the Sharps rifle from the saddle scabbard and slipped a cartridge into the chamber. Spirit Talker and the others quickly nocked arrows in preparation for taking on the bear. To make matters more challenging, the bear's mate arrived on the scene. We now faced a male likely weighing in at better than six hundred pounds and his sow weighing a hundred and fifty or so pounds less. In short, both were big. Cubs were likely nearby. Claws? Long. Teeth? Huge.

The male stood and glared at us. He was nearly nine feet tall. He turned from the deer to face what he figured was a threat. He was correct. He released a roar that even Big Red trembled at. My big stallion finally steadied enough for me to aim the Sharps. I dared not miss. Bears on the run were exceptionally fast. There'd be no time to reload, and the arrows from my companions would likely serve as mere annoyances. I'd heard of trappers with flintlocks years back needing as many as a dozen musket balls to bring down a big grizzly. Of all the natural predators feared by bears, the wolf pretty much topped the list. Blessedly, the grizzly was distracted for a split second by the appearance of Zeb and his pack. But the bear wasn't to be dissuaded by the snarls from Zeb's pack. He was hungry and angry at all the distractions from his meal. He looked ready to add our packhorse to his meal. The frightened packhorse pranced about despite the weight of the deer on his back.

"Hey! Hey, bear!" I hollered in an attempt to distract him from the deer. The grizzly bared his great teeth at me and let out a huge roar. He stood even taller and then unwittingly turned to give me a full-frontal target. I aimed and squeezed the trigger. An explosion rent the air. The round plowed dead center into the bear's chest and out his back, leaving a considerable hole in its path. The bear staggered at the impact and bellowed. He was also struck by at least four arrows unleashed by my

Comanche companions. The great beast paused and swatted a great paw at where my bullet had struck him and flailed at the arrows. He began struggling to breathe. The great bear's pause would cost him dearly, as I slipped a second round into the Sharps. Once again, I aimed, took a breath, and squeezed the trigger. He tumbled over in a heap.

The sow let loose a fearsome snarl at Zeb and sniffed at her mate. Had she been human, she'd surely have shed tears. She looked sort of beseechingly at us, gave a sad sort of whimper, and ambled off to protect her cubs.

Our hunt had turned into quite an adventure. We'd happened upon the remains of an Apache attack, bagged five deer and a wild boar, and now were blessed with a grizzly. The grizzly was highly valued by the Indians as much for the wonderful fur blanket it made and its decorative claws and fangs, but for its fat that was turned into a coveted lubricant. I had gifted Spirit Talker's father, Buffalo Hump, with the bearskin from an earlier kill, and he'd understandably been very appreciative.

Spirit Talker looked at me. "Gun kill. Bear belong to Pohya Isa," he declared to our hunting party companions that I had the honor of the kill and earned the prize of the claws and hide.

We now had a considerable load to take back to the village so we built a travois to handle the carcasses.

———

WE RETURNED to the village with the deer, the wild boar, and the bear. We saw no Apache, though they might have seen us and known better than to risk an attack. We shared our adventure at the council fire on the evening of our return. The message of hateful Whites and marauding Apache sat heavily upon everyone. The success of our hunting would be told again at future council fires, though it would surely be embellished as having required ever-braver action on our part. After feasting, we returned to our teepees.

With my belly full and mind still dealing with the grizzly, I sat cross-legged, staring thoughtfully into the fire in our teepee that evening. My thinking drifted to the three men who'd been attacked.

"What matter?" asked Blue Flower, as she sat beside me.

"Men hate men for color of skin. It's so sad."

She sat beside me. "Jack strong *sunipu*. Do much."

I looked into Blue Flower's beautiful eyes. I was a lucky man to have her in my life. God had surely blessed me. "Are you happy here with your *numunuu*?" I was implying a comparison with the life at Rising Cross Ranch. Was the life of the Plains Indian better than the civilization evolving with the culture brought by the White settlers? It was quite obviously a tough question. She had family in both worlds—as did I.

She looked around the interior of the teepee. The twins and Peter were sleeping behind a buffalo hide screen. "Old ways go away," she said. "Comanche must learn *tosa* ways." She paused in thought, and I kept silent. "Some *tosa* good, some bad. Comanche good and bad."

I nodded. "We must all be free to choose. Some want to take choice from us." I stroked my chin thoughtfully. "It is up to us to know truth, to make choices for good. Our freedom, our future, depend upon it." I knew that a strong family rooted in God's truth was key to survival. It had already come to my thinking that family was the essential core element of a free society, as it served as the bedrock of civilization. We had to build our families on the rock of truth, since building on the sands of lies washed families away when deluged with the storms of diversity.

Blue Flower smiled. Peter whimpered. She got up, brought him back to the warmth of the fire, and began nursing him. She looked deeply into my eyes. "Love help *numunuu...*" She struggled for the words. "Help *numunuu* be brave to speak the truth. Evil spirit no stop truth. Blue Flower love Jack speak truth."

I smiled and lovingly kissed her lightly. "Blue Flower is right. It make us strong to fight for what's right. It also gives the humility to forgive those who have wronged us. It is the way to overcome our differences and move forward." I watched how tenderly she cradled Peter. This was the love that empowered me, magnifying the faith I had in God. God was my ultimate trust. "We go home soon."

She smiled and nodded.

Zeb strolled in and nuzzled Peter with his wet nose. While I feared he was becoming more pet dog than companion wolf, I knew that the instincts of the wild were deep within his soul. He'd surely proven it many times. I reached out and stroked Zeb.

Blue Flower finished feeding Peter and lay him back in his cradle. She locked on to my eyes. The deepest of loves called from her dark eyes. For the moment, I would forget that, one way or another, we must face up to the challenges and dangers posed by those that held deeply rooted prejudices and hatreds.

FIVE
THE WHITE FORELOCK

SPRING HAD ARRIVED. The twins were babbling a mix of English and Comanche and tottering around the village. Blue Flower and I decided the time had come to take our family back to Rising Cross Ranch.

The night before our departure, Spirit Talker and Prairie Flower came to our teepee to share the evening meal.

It was likely the last time I'd be eating a meal while sitting cross-legged before a fire in a teepee. The meal was scrumptious as befitting a feast for our hosts. We fully enjoyed the moment, as the air filled with a mix of English and Comanche combined with the laughter of small children.

Soon, it was time for a discussion that called for the ceremonial pipe, the one used with serious talk. We intuitively knew what the topic would be. I smiled thoughtfully as I stuffed tobacco in the bowl, lit it, and took a couple of long pulls. The pipe smoke mingled with that of the fire and was drawn upward. "We face great danger. Danger must be faced. Losing the freedom to speak truth is at stake." This was a strong opening statement. I passed the pipe to Spirit Talker.

He took a thoughtful pull on the pipe and sent a column of smoke upward toward the vent flap. "Pohya Isa brave. Mukwooru must stay. Buffalo Hump not well." He sighed with a decided longing. He saw adventure ahead, adventure of the sort we'd tackled together many times. He passed the pipe back to me.

I drew in the sweet smoke and watched it curl upward as I exhaled. "We pray for Buffalo Hump." I smiled reassuringly. "Mukwooru and Pohya Isa meet in two moons where Pinta Trail meet Guadalupe River," I stated with finality. We recognized that such a rendezvous would be intended to make life decisions.

Spirit Talker took the pipe from me and took a pull. "Comanche way," he hesitated with a sad look on his face. "Comanche way is old way. If no change, many Comanche die." Then he stared at me. "Slavery bad. Many *tosa* die." It was an observation and perhaps a dire prediction. He was about to hand the pipe back to me when he paused. "But…Whites keep coming. Many die, more come." He had spoken a hard truth. There was no bitterness, simply recognition of a truth. The civilization of the White man was vastly larger and more culturally advanced than the Comanche. Whites carried more powerful weapons, mostly fended off the diseases that killed Indians, tilled the soil with greater productivity, spawned larger families, raised far more livestock, lived longer, built permanent settlements, held to a God-based system of law and order, and most held an abiding faith in a powerful, loving God. By comparison, the Red man was of an age long past that had changed little over thousands of years. The White man's system of land ownership was totally foreign to the Redman. The very idea of placing tribes on reservations with defined boundaries was a concept that confounded the Indians.

I nodded, as Spirit Talker handed me the pipe. After pausing thoughtfully, I grasped it in both hands and raised it upward ceremonially. We had spoken of the realities of a world that was more untamed than civilized. We intuitively knew what the future held. While I would strive to help fashion an ever-better life, we were all too aware of having to deal with mankind's often sinful nature. I looked from Spirit Talker to Prairie Flower to Blue Flower. "We go with rising sun," I stated matter-of-factly.

The women were resigned to the eventuality of Blue Flower and me returning to Rising Cross Ranch. They also were well aware of the adventurous nature of their spouses. They were ever-amazed at our willingness to take on the risks of the unexpected and our commitment to fighting for the truth.

"Meet in two moons," reiterated Spirit Talker.

———

WE HAD STRUCK the teepee before dawn. It would be stored here at the Comanche village.

Spirit Talker and Prairie Flower arose early to see us off.

I helped Blue Flower mount her pony and secured the cradle boards for our children. Our outfit included a packhorse and two extra ponies. Spirit Talker figured to ride with us a spell, then head back. Two Comanche warriors would guide and guard us so far as the Pinta Trail. I was about to mount Big Red when a voice interrupted me.

"Pohya Isa no say goodbye?" Buffalo Hump was ill

but had found the strength to see us off on our journey home. He emerged from his teepee with the bearskin robe I'd given him a couple of years back draped over his shoulders.

The chief could now be best described as elderly. He bore the wrinkles and scars of a legendary life as a warrior and leader of the Penateka Comanche. Buffalo Hump limped over to me. His right hand grasped my shoulder, and his eyes searched mine. "Go with *Taa Narumi*." He bowed his head slightly in acknowledgment of God. "*Pohya Isa onaa*." The once-mighty chief had called me his son. He hugged me and smiled. "Pohya Isa always welcome." By now, I'd become accustomed to the mix of English and Comanche and was impressed at how well the chief spoke. It was an emotional moment, as he had touched me deeply. I had saved the life of his son, married his daughter, brought him three grandchildren, and saved his warriors from sure defeat at the hands of Rip Ford's Texas Rangers. Buffalo Hump's eyes never left mine. He reached deep within the folds of the bearskin robe. He presented me with an exquisitely tanned buffalo hide with painted images telling the story of my brief life journey with the Penateka Comanche.

Spirit Talker nodded approvingly.

I heard Blue Flower gasp with surprise.

This was a huge moment. My loyalty, respect, and strength—my strong *sunipu*—had fully earned the trust of the Comanche chief. I had become a Penateka Comanche and the son of a chief. My life was commemorated on a robe.

Buffalo Hump smiled and motioned for me to mount up. As a no-nonsense chief and Comanche warrior, he didn't believe in long goodbyes. Actions spoke louder than words and his actions that morning had spoken for him.

I knew that I'd treasure his gift for the rest of my days.

We were soon headed eastward, following the south bank of the Pedernales River. It would be a two-day journey in the still-chilly air of mid-March.

————

THE COUNTRY WAS raw and rugged, but we'd become accustomed to it. As we plodded along ever mindful of possible lurking threats, I thought back to how my life had changed since growing to my early teen years on my folks' farm in Pennsylvania. In the intervening years, I'd become a man toughened in ways no teen back east could hope to attain. At nineteen years old, I had a wife, three children, a thriving ranch, loyal friends, and had packed enough adventure into my brief life to exceed a lifetime of experiences of most men. Yes, I had made plenty of enemies, but I'd managed to bring many of them to faith in God. Who knew what the future might hold? God knew. Would Gordon Small keep conjuring lies about me to sell newspapers? Would Rolf Schultz stir up more trouble for whatever evil ends he sought? Would Sheriff Hoffman be an ally or an enemy? Could I help more slaves escape to freedom?

We rode on, ever-considerate of the capricious nature of the frontier and its dangers. Despite our Comanche escort, this was country in which Utes, Arapaho, Kiowa, Apache, and other not-so-friendly Comanche tribes roamed. A few careless moments could spell disaster for the unwary traveler.

We were always mindful of the sky. Its azure vastness

during the day and shadowy majesty at night could warn of impending threats. Importantly, the sky served as a guide. At night, keeping the North Star in sight helped keep us on track, while during daylight hours, the sun became reference. In the absence of sun or stars, something as simple as moss growing on the north side of a tree trunk or an outstanding landmark served as worthy substitutions.

God's commandments were always in play, but consciousness of my surroundings was a law—a commandment, if you will—of the frontier. The wind blew—was there an unusual scent? The landscape spoke —were you listening or just hearing? Sight, smell, touch, hear, taste—my senses were constantly challenged.

We reached the head of the Pinta Trail which we'd follow from the Pedernales River to the Guadalupe River. We were yet a long day's journey from Rising Cross Ranch. We watched the two Comanche warriors fan out to our left and right. They would follow us until we reached home, ensuring that no harm came to Buffalo Hump's adopted son and to his daughter and grandchildren. I sensed that there were likely more of his warriors about than the two we were aware of.

It was an unusually windy day. As we headed south, I detected an out-of-the-ordinary smell being carried in the dust. Big Red sensed it, too, as his ears pricked up. Horses can pick up sounds beyond the range of human hearing, so I trusted in Big Red's reaction. I dismounted as much to rest Big Red as to concentrate on the trail ahead. I slipped my Sharps rifle from its scabbard, glancing back at Blue Flower as I did it. She was watching me intently. I hoped our Comanche companions also sensed what I felt to be impending danger.

Soon enough, the faint sound of hoofbeats reached

my ears. Whomever was riding was pushing their horses hard. There were parts of the trail that defied a horse moving faster than a walk, but this was a wider, flatter portion. I led Blue Flower and our horses off the trail into a stand of live oak. They were out of sight to all but the practiced eye. I climbed back aboard Big Red and sat with my rifle across the pommel of my saddle. We waited. My experienced eyes could just make out one of our Comanche guards high on a bluff overlooking the trail. The other was likely behind me, and there were surely more. Zeb sat alertly beside Big Red. If trouble was coming—and my senses told me it was trouble—they'd get more than they'd bargained for.

Around the bend in the trail ahead came a half dozen riders. The leader was none other than Rolf Schultz riding that familiar black horse with the white forelock. I asked myself what on earth he might be up to riding so hard toward Fredericksburg. At the pace he was traveling, his horses would be spent sooner than later. Were they fleeing something or someone?

Schultz's band was coming ever closer, and I held high hopes that he'd pass us by undetected. That turned out to be wishful thinking. A herd of deer darted across the trail, causing Schultz and his men to halt in a cloud of dust and hail of loose rocks. As it was, a leaping buck knocked one of Schultz's men clear of his saddle and into a cactus.

The man stood up with a cactus branch stuck to his backside and happened to look straight at me. "Boss... look!" he shouted and pointed at me.

By now, Schultz had his cayuse under control. His eyes followed to where his man pointed.

What could I do? I smiled at Schultz and tipped my hat—all the while keeping my right hand gripped firmly around the receiver of my Sharps. My finger flicked gently at the trigger.

"Get him, men!" shouted Schultz to his gang.

"Zeb! Go!" I shouted.

Zeb took off and launched himself at Schultz, knocking him clean off his horse.

I dug my heels into Big Red's sides and was near instantly on top of Schultz. He had no time to react, and the fall had knocked the wind from him. I leaped from my saddle and stood with the muzzle of my Sharps stuck in Schultz's belly. My finger was wrapped around the trigger. A squeeze, and this evil soul would meet his destiny. His men dared not attack.

Time froze.

Schultz looked up at me pleadingly.

I was trying my best to cool off. "Where you from, Schultz?" I dearly wanted to squeeze the trigger. Mercy, Jack...mercy...mercy—the words kept floating through my mind. The man didn't deserve an ounce of mercy.

Schultz's men loitered to the side, uncertain as to what to do. Their cayuses pranced nervously, and riders looked about in a state of near panic, as a half dozen Comanche with nocked arrows and a pack of wolves led by Zeb held them at bay.

"Where you from?" I said, pressing the muzzle harder into his gut. "Talk, or your guts will be spread across all creation."

"Atlanta," responded Schultz with a shaky voice.

"Who sent you?"

"Don't know," he replied.

"You came all the way to Texas from Georgia and don't know who sent you?" I was incredulous, but sensed that the sniveling excuse for a human was telling the truth. I pulled the revolver from his holster, then rooted through his vest and relieved him of a Deringer stuffed in an inside pocket. All the while, the muzzle of the Sharps remained nestled in his midsection. Satisfied that I'd disarmed him, I backed off and motioned him to get up. "What did whoever sent you order you to do?" It was sort of what they call a rhetorical question, as the answer was obvious.

Schultz arose shakily, as the fall had taken the starch from him. "They send me money. I stir up hate against abolitionists."

Evil as he was, the man was forthright in revealing his mission. "Why?"

"They want a war."

Again, he was being straightforward. Can't say I could blame him. At his core, he was a coward. I was beginning to consider what to do with this sorry excuse for a human. "Tell your men to lose their guns."

Schultz looked over and quickly realized the gravity of his situation. That and the muzzle of my rifle still aimed at him served as convincing arguments for following my order. "Men! Drop your weapons," he ordered.

There was the thud of rifles and revolvers dropping to the ground.

My Comanche escorts and Zeb remained ever watchful.

"So, you stir up hateful rumors about me and place my family in danger. What should I do with you, Rolf Schultz?"

Schultz's eyes darted about at my considering his fate.

Was he salvageable? Was he another Brawny Jones that could be saved? I sensed a deeply embedded evil in him. Despite his straight answers to my questions—all under threat of imminent execution—he was a man who seemed to relish his assignment to spew racial hatred across the land. In my brief experience with life, I had learned that something is always lost by sin, even when it is forgiven—even when mercy is bestowed. I had the sense that if I let Schultz go free, he'd quickly return to spreading his evil. Then again, I was not judge and jury—not even out here on the frontier. I felt a chill wind, and it gave me an idea.

Our Comanche escorts were waiting patiently. I gave Schultz a look that might have melted steel. "Don't move a muscle," I ordered. I eased over to the nearest of the Comanche and directed him to lead Blue Flower up the trail. I didn't want her to see what I was about to do to Schultz and his men. I waited until he had led her out of sight. While arrows were still aimed at Schultz's gang, I slipped my rifle back into its scabbard. At close quarters, my Colt revolver would do just fine. I then proceeded to gather up the weapons lying about the ground and unload them. Nobody moved a muscle. I placed all the ammunition in a leather sack and hung it from my saddle horn. I asked another Comanche to gather our prisoners' cayuses and told him they were theirs to keep.

Our prisoners looked panicky as the horses were rounded up.

"What are you going to do?" said Schultz with a quivering voice. He watched as his black stallion with the white forelock became a Comanche prize.

The chill wind swept in again. The temperature was dropping. "I could leave y'all to my friends here," I said with an arm sweep toward the Comanche and nod toward Zeb. I punctuated it with a slicing motion across my forehead.

Schultz glanced about furtively as though seeking some sort of escape from whatever fate I had in mind.

"I could do what my Texas Ranger friends have been known to do," I mused aloud. I made a choking motion as in lynching. "But I'm a God-fearing man, Mr. Schultz."

There was momentary relief in his eyes.

I swept the gang with the muzzle of my Colt. My finger remained on the trigger. "I could simply finish y'all off. No one would know."

Panic returned to the captives.

"Take off your boots." I waved the muzzle at them.

The wind picked up as they removed their boots.

"Remove your clothes," I ordered.

"We'll freeze," uttered one of the prisoners.

An explosion rent the air as I fired the Colt into the ground beside the man. Schultz gave me a look, recognizing that I had one less bullet in my gun. "Don't even think it, Mr. Schultz," I said with a look to the arrows still aimed at them.

The prisoners all stripped.

"Now, put your boots back on." I could barely contain a laugh at the sight of six naked men shivering in the cold with only their boots on.

Schultz laid a decidedly evil stare on me.

"Better to hold no grudge, Mr. Schultz. This here is the law of the frontier, and you're lucky I'm a merciful man. If you come near me ever again, you'll be taking your last breath. Do we understand each other?"

Schultz nodded. "Yeah," he managed through chattering teeth. If he could have mustered it, he'd likely have given me a look that could kill.

"Y'all are likely close enough to Fredericksburg to make it by nightfall. If y'all keep moving, the chill won't be quite so bad." I thought on them crossing the Pedernales River all naked in the March chill. The men turned and began walking northward. I mounted Big Red and proceeded up the trail to catch up with Blue Flower. Zeb hesitated but then followed me much to the relief of the men. I reckoned I hadn't seen the last of Schultz. I'd made our situation personal.

As I rode up the trail, one of the Comanche led the black stallion with the white forelock to me. He handed me the reins and signed that it was my prize. The irony of possessing Schultz's horse wasn't lost on me. It would serve as a reminder, especially since he—coward that he was—would surely return to fetch the cayuse.

It occurred to me that I still didn't know why Schultz had been heading toward Fredericksburg. I could only assume that he aimed to stir up hate and discontent among the German immigrants. Given what I knew of their inclinations about slavery, I figured he'd have a rough time of it.

SIX
ANGRY MOMMA

BLUE FLOWER DIDN'T ASK what I'd done to Schultz and his gang. She knew me well enough to have figured it out without asking.

As we turned south from the Guadalupe River but two miles from our home, my eyes were drawn to the herd grazing in our north pasture. Before me was a veritable sea of horns glistening in the rays of sunlight. Longhorns! Brindle, red, brown, spotted! They were an ornery lot, ready to fight at anything they found annoying. Horn spreads ranged from five to as much as nine feet tip to tip, depending on the age of the beast. And they all bore the Rising Cross brand. Come spring, Shorty would head them north.

We were greeted with great joy upon our arrival. Will and Kate were expecting another child and Isaac and Sarah had welcomed a second child to their family. Shorty had taken Buck with him to Kerrville, and my now twelve-year-old brother had his first puppy love with a storekeeper's daughter. It didn't matter to young Buck that she was fourteen—an older woman. Brawny and Hardy cowboyed, when they weren't making improvements to Rising Cross Ranch.

It occurred to me that I needed to find some escaped slaves, if I was to continue my mission and keep my underground railroad functioning. For better or worse, for right or wrong, slaves were considered chattel property by those that held them in bondage. I refused to call them owners anymore, as it didn't sit right with me that any man should own another. Despite my efforts, I lamented that they were as a mere piece of dust in the vastness of the prairie. There were hundreds of thousands of slaves, and I had managed to spirit only three to freedom. While I appreciated the faith that Blue Flower had in my efforts, I desperately wanted to do more—much more.

Within two weeks of our return, I seized the opportunity to purchase a neighbor's fifty-thousand-acre ranch northwest of us. This brought out holdings to about a hundred and ten thousand acres. It was a long way from Richard King's massive million-acre spread to our south, but it was significant. While I still wasn't old enough to vote in Texas, my growing wealth in terms of land and livestock translated into increased influence upon the world around me. I hadn't truly tested that influence but figured I'd get my chance sooner than later.

We appreciated the arrival of warmer weather and longer days. The creeks were near overflowing and flowers were blooming in all their multi-hued glory. Seemed that every day we welcomed new livestock into the world. We'd heard nary a word from vigilantes, and encounters with Indians mostly occurred deeper into the frontier. Life seemed so good.

Blue Flower and I sat one morning at breakfast, savoring a mighty fine coffee, it was a special brew she'd blended. I looked over the lip of my cup to find her staring intently at me. It was as though she was trying to reach into my soul. We'd frolicked a bit during the night, but her gaze seemed to bore in unimpeded. I found myself shifting a tad uncomfortably. "What?" I finally blurted.

"Ecclesiastes," she responded. Turns out that she'd begun reading the Bible. "God speak of hunting great wealth...only find no happiness at end. Like chasing wind. Is hollow reward."

I didn't know where she'd come up with some of her words, but she sure as shooting was right. She was telling me not to get too big for my britches. I took a long sip of coffee, ignoring it being just hot enough to burn my lips.

"Jack strong *sunipu*." Her expression turned from penetration to compassion. "Jack quiet *sunipu* like *hoikwa aruka*." She was telling me to be stealthy, to exercise my strong medicine as though stalking deer. These were wise words.

I gave her a knowing smile.

"Day clear...warm," she cooed.

We hadn't taken one of our rides up to my old fishing spot on the Guadalupe since returning from our stay with the Penateka Comanche. "I'll saddle Big Red and the mare." Left unsaid was that she'd pull together some sustenance for our tryst. My sister Kate would keep an eye on the boys.

It didn't take me long to ready our horses. Big Red was especially frisky and anxious for a ride. Zeb appeared seemingly from nowhere. As usual, my wolf companion would serve as sentry, warning us should a threat arise.

Blue Flower's words of wisdom referencing Ecclesiastes still hung with me. I dared not let my hunger for influence and power, its close relative, overtake my mission. In my brief experience with life, I'd observed that unbridled power bred carelessness resulted in unhappy endings. It wouldn't do to risk my family by using my influence to impose and thereby flaunt my anti-slavery beliefs. Patience was a key virtue to embrace. Time was my ally, despite my fears of a national firestorm looming near at hand.

I let Shorty know where we were heading. He knew to keep an eye out but not come so close as to impose upon our intimate time together.

———

AS WE DREW near our favorite spot near the river, we were serenaded by the desperate braying of a longhorn cow. Whatever was going on didn't sound so good. We urged our horses to a canter and quickly arrived on the scene. The combination of spring thaw and a couple of heavy rain showers had created a muddy area along the south bank of the river.

Low and behold, a calf not more than a couple of weeks old was mired in the slop. As it struggled, it sank ever deeper. The mother, a brindle with about a seven-foot horn spread, was beside herself with grief and had managed to sink her forelegs into the mud.

Blue Flower and I looked at each other knowingly. So much for our romantic tryst.

"We're going to pull these critters from the mire, sweetheart."

She gave me a helpless sort of look. Cowpoking wasn't exactly her thing.

"Just do as I say. It won't be easy." I tried to sound reassuring, as I climbed down from Big Red. "Hand me that lasso," I said, pointing to the rope looped over her saddle horn.

The cow was none too happy about our approaching her helpless calf. Reading longhorn dispositions was an uncertain proposition. They might be so docile they'd let you hug and kiss them or take an aggressive, nasty turn and give you what for. Mama longhorn was acting somewhere in between those extremes. Fortunately, there was a good six feet between the cow and her calf, and that gave me barely enough space to work. There were cowpokes that would just let poor trapped critters like the calf flounder about until they struggled themselves to death. That wasn't my nature.

I spoke real easy-like, as I approached. "Nice cow, going to save your baby." I repeated it over and over. I had a plan in mind, as I carried the lasso from Blue Flower's cayuse in my hand and the one from my own looped over my shoulder. I expect I wasn't approaching gently enough and speaking easy enough, as the cow let out an angry bellow that only a mother protecting her young could let loose. She was now in full attack temperament. If her legs weren't stuck, she'd have had her way with me, and it would have been none too pleasant.

I stepped out so far as I dared into the muck and managed to loop the end of one of the lassos around the rump of the calf. I handed it up to Blue Flower. "Wrap this around your saddle horn but don't pull yet." I took another step and was able to get the loop of my second lasso around the little fella's neck. I eased on out, mounted Big Red, and took a couple of wraps of the rope around my own saddle horn.

Meanwhile, momma longhorn was getting angrier by the second. She was not appreciating our work at all.

"Okay, let's pull the little fellow out real slow," I said to Blue Flower. We eased our cayuses very gently until the ropes grew taut and then ever-so-slowly eased the calf from the mud. Poor guy was so tired he offered nary a whimper. He soon stood on wobbly legs but solid ground.

Momma kept reminding us of her unhappiness. She was seriously ungrateful.

Blue Flower dismounted and tenderly loosened the lassos from the calf. She surprised me, as she re-coiled the ropes like an experienced cowboy. She handed one up to me before gently guiding the calf to one side so it didn't walk into the bog again. The poor little guy began bleating for his momma.

I took a long hard look at the ingrate cow. She still bellowed up a storm, but her forelegs remained stuck fast in the muck. I threw a loop around her horns and put Big Red into reverse. We began some serious pulling. There was eventually a big sucking sound as the brindle cow came free. I managed to make enough slack in the rope to shuck it from her horns. She stared balefully at me, as I went about gathering my rope while keeping an eye on her.

The unappreciative beast pawed the ground. Her stare turned decidedly nasty. She was still ready to attack, as her slow, bovine mind still hadn't accommodated the fact that I wasn't a threat. There was perhaps thirty or so feet between us. She let out a horrendous bellow and gathered herself to charge. Just as she was about to launch, her calf pulled free of Blue Flower and stood directly between momma cow and me. Amazingly, the fire left her eyes pretty much immediately. She eased over to her calf and began licking him. Next thing, she led him off a few yards, and he began feeding. She looked over her shoulder as if to say, *No problem, cowboy.* A *thank you* might have been welcome.

I looked over at Blue Flower. Her gentle, admiring smile spoke volumes. "You ready to picnic, sweetheart?"

She smiled that smile that melted my knees.

We dismounted and spread our picnic fixings on a blanket under our favorite tree overlooking the Guadalupe River. Other than the mud on my boots, a passerby might never have suspected that we'd just saved a couple of longhorns.

Eventually, momma and calf ambled off.

SEVEN
DEADLY NEWS

THE TIME WAS GROWING ripe to be driving longhorns north again. I sat on the gallery along the front of our house, sipping a cup of coffee, as I thought on where to find a couple of escaped slaves to train for the drive. My senses, the ones that came alive when trouble lurked, stirred. Those feelings were validated by the expression on Hardy's face upon his arrival from patrolling the north pasture.

He remained in the saddle. Usually, my hands would dismount, as we made it a practice of offering coffee when they brought news. "Got a problem, boss," he stated with concern.

I stood and took a step to the railing. "Problem?" I asked.

"Figure you ain't gonna like it." He seemed at a bit of a loss. "That black horse with the white forelock is missing."

"You certain?" I sought confirmation.

"Looked everywhere," he said with a resigned shake of his head.

I finished my coffee in a single gulp. While I trusted Hardy, I figured to see for myself. "Get Shorty and Brawny," I directed. "I'll meet y'all at the barn."

I saddled Big Red in a heartbeat and led him out to meet the men. "Where's Brawny?" I asked upon seeing Hardy and Shorty.

Shorty shrugged. "He done rode out this mornin', boss," he added with considerable concern.

This worried me a might. Those senses of mine now spun up right high. I looked down at Zeb. He gave me that cock-of-the-head look of his that said he sensed my concern. I had retrieved one of Brawny's bandannas from the bunkhouse and gave Zeb a sniff at it.

Buck rode up and joined us out of curiosity over what was going happening. "Y'all looking for Brawny? I saw him head out early. I was fixing to take a ride around the south range, and he waved to me as he headed north."

I shook my head. "What are y'all thinking?! With all the hate and discontent about the countryside, we had made the decision to only go out in pairs. Pray to God nothing's happened to Brawny."

The three looked appropriately hangdog at not following the rules.

About this time, Will emerged from his cabin. "What's happening?" he called out.

"Horse is missing and so is Brawny," responded Shorty.

"Give me a minute, and I'll join y'all." Will headed for the corral and was soon saddled up.

Will joining us would give us five men making the search. There was no point in any further scolding, so I turned Big Red northward and led the men out.

We crossed the Guadalupe and gathered to plan our search. "We need to spread out. Fire a single shot, when you find any sign. Fire two, if you find Brawny." We spread out and began our search, concentrating mostly on arroyos and tree lines. The landscape was hilly, so any search was a tad challenging. Clear skies eased our task.

I was about to head due north, when Zeb gave me a whimper and headed in a northwesterly direction. I reckoned he might have caught Brawny's scent, so Big Red and I trotted on behind him.

I rode perhaps two miles to the edge of a stand of live oak. Zeb barked as though he'd found something. I drew my revolver. Among the trees, the Sharps rifle would be awkward. About fifty feet into the trees stood Brawny's saddled horse. I went to shield my eyes from the sun, as I looked about for sign. My eyes happened to catch the glint of metal on the ground beside a nearby fallen tree. I took a sweeping scan of the area for any lurking threat and slipped from my saddle. Upon closer inspection, the metal objects were shell casings. There were three, and the area beside the tree was tamped down as though someone had been kneeling there. I examined the log, and whoever had been there had rested his weapon where bark had been scuffed. Shielding my eyes from the sun, I gazed out into the vast prairie. I could see a small herd of our horses grazing lazily in the distance. Ambush crossed my mind, but more likely, it was an impromptu situation. It looked as though someone had been figuring to steal a certain horse and Brawny happened upon the scene.

I heard another bark from Zeb. He was prancing excitedly about a few feet from Brawny's horse. I could just about make out the outline of a body lying askew. I fired two shots to alert Shorty and the others.

I strode over to examine Zeb's find. Sure enough, it was Brawny, and he was dead. My heart stopped. I had grown ever closer to the rough former slave catcher. He'd found Christ, become my friend, and here he lay slain by some murderer's bullets. From what I could see, two of the bushwhacker's slugs had struck him in the chest. His rifle was lying close by. I examined it. Brawny had managed at least one shot. There was no telling whether he'd hit anything.

Buck arrived first. "What did you find, big brother?"

I was about to respond when the others came galloping in. I waited for them to dismount and join us. "Brawny's dead. Somebody bushwhacked him. From what I can put together, Brawny must have come upon whoever stole the black stallion with the white forelock. Brawny likely tried to stop the horse thief and was shot for his trouble. I found three casings over yonder." I pointed to the log. "Brawny got off at least one shot, but there's no sign of his hitting the thief."

"Sorry about Brawny, boss," consoled Hardy. "Let's scout around and see whether the killer left any evidence," he suggested, drawing upon his Texas Ranger experience. "Careful where y'all step," he added.

I ruffled Zeb's mane and gave him a treat. He'd done a great job of finding Brawny. He'd even had a taste of him in a past encounter, yet had realized that the redeemed Brawny was no longer a threat.

There'd yet be time to mourn our friend's death. I scanned the forested area thoughtfully. Where might someone on the run be most likely to head? I searched for hoofprints, but the ground near the shooter's position had been trampled and revealed nothing. There was a natural break in the trees about fifty yards away, so I walked toward it with Big Red and Zeb following. Shorty and the men had fanned out among the trees. I was focused on the ground before me, when a strip of black cloth lying near some rocks caught my attention. I examined it closely. Blood. There was blood on the cloth, and it was fresh. It had been torn off and possibly used to staunch blood from a wound. It seemed that Brawny had hit his attacker.

I placed the cloth in a sack and continued toward the opening in the trees. I finally picked up the hoofprints of two horses. The thief had ridden away with the stallion in tow. I didn't figure to trail the killer on my own, plus he'd have at least a three-hour head start. The tracks headed southward toward Bandera. If I were a betting man—and I'm not—I'd bet that the horse thief was Rolf Schultz or someone in his employ.

I headed back to where Brawny still lay beside his horse. Once everyone had reassembled, we placed Brawny over his horse's saddle and headed back to arrange for his funeral and figure what to do next. I shared my suspicions on the way home. I wondered how much help Sheriff Hoffman would be? He'd ask for hard evidence. A wounded man and whatever that piece of bloodied cloth had been torn from likely qualified.

———

ROLF SCHULTZ LEANED FORWARD and gently swished the whiskey around the glass. The amber liquid reflected the glow of the kerosene lamp on the wall. He savored a slow sip. "Now, what was it you were saying, Gordon?"

Small quaffed the last residue of beer in his glass and swiped his sleeve across his mouth. "That killing out on O'Toole place is riling a few folks."

"Don't matter. It bothering you?" countered Schultz.

"I just report the news," replied Small.

Schultz laid a judgmental stare on the newspaper-man. "What are you trying to tell me?"

Small appeared momentarily distracted. "Gotta use the privy. Tell you when I get back." With that, he stood and hurried out the back door of the saloon, leaving his coat hanging over the back of the chair.

The combination of Schultz's suspicious mind and outright curiosity got the best of him. With a look at the saloon back door, he reached into the inside pocket of Small's jacket and lifted out the reporter's notebook. He flipped through a few pages, especially the most recent entries. His brows came together in anger. He returned the notebook just as he caught Small returning.

Small resumed his seat. "Where were we?"

"No matter, Gordon. I have some business to tend to." He forced a smile. "I'll catch up with you later." He hailed the barkeep to refill Small's glass.

"Why, thanks kindly," offered Small as he watched Schultz depart.

———

IN BRAWNY, I had found a brother in faith. He'd read the Bible I had given him and turned from his bounty-hunting slave catcher days to become a valuable part of Rising Cross Ranch. We buried him right proper with a cross at the head of the grave. I would treasure memories of the man, even our less-than-savory encounters wherein I showed him mercy for his sinful ways. He'd be missed. I would miss him dearly.

I decided that only Hardy and me would head to Bandera. Too many of us riding into town might be taken as a threat.

Blue Flower was deeply concerned. Once again,

violence had found its way onto Rising Cross Ranch and there I was about to head to Bandera courting trouble. "Jack, be careful," she pleaded, as I sat my saddle. She handed me a sack of jerky, pemmican, and some bear sign. Hardy and I would eat well on our journey.

"If we're not back in three days, send Shorty, Will, and Buck for us," I reminded her. With that and a farewell kiss, we headed on out for Bandera. The sky looked a tad rain-heavy, but we'd brought slickers along so didn't especially worry about that. If rain got heavy, crossing the Medina River could get dicey.

We needn't have worried, as the ride to Bandera went smoothly. We encountered nary a soul on the trail, though there was always the feeling that we were watched. We kept in mind that it was Comanche territory.

As we approached the outskirts of Bandera, we reined in our cayuses. "Keep your eyes peeled, Hardy. I don't reckon they'll be welcoming us with open arms."

We instinctively checked the loads in our guns. Perhaps, that in itself was a sad commentary on the state of affairs.

"Let's stop by Klappenbach's store first." I figured that he'd have a pretty fair handle on the latest goings on in Bandera.

There were a few folks about, as Bandera was a thriving hub of cattle activity, and cowboys gravitated to the town. Also, there was still a thriving business in cedar shingles. No one seemed to pay attention to us as we rode easy-like up the main street toward Klappenbach's store. As we reined in at his place, my peripheral vision caught someone take a hard look at us and run off. That seemed just a tad suspicious, but I wasn't going to overreact.

We hitched our horses to the rail in front of Klappenbach's store and dismounted with wary eyes scanning our surroundings. I wouldn't forget the last time we were here with Schultz's armed henchman positioned on nearby rooftops. I led the way into the store.

"Is August home?" I asked the young lady behind the counter. It appeared that Klappenbach had hired some help.

"He's in the," she began.

"Well, Jack O'Toole! Welcome!" boomed August Klappenbach. "I thought I heard your voice." He charged forward and delivered a bear hug. It was a decidedly different greeting from our last encounter, when he and his wife Stella were hiding inside the church to avoid potential gunplay on the streets.

"Great to see you, too," I responded. I broke free. "You remember Hardy here?" I said, motioning toward my companion.

"What brings y'all to Bandera?" asked Klappenbach.

"Been a murder and horse thievery out at Rising Cross, August," I advised.

"More killing?" Klappenbach lamented.

"Figured I'd get the latest on goings on here from you before I visit Sheriff Hoffman."

"Y'all have a suspect?"

I nodded.

Klappenbach shook his head. "That fella Schultz is still spreading hate around the countryside. He's paying that newspaper fella Gordon Small to write pro-slavery news. There are a lot of thinly veiled threats going around."

"What about the sheriff?" I asked.

"Hoffman is pretty much sticking to the middle

ground. He's politically savvy enough to keep his nose out of trouble," observed Klappenbach.

I rubbed my chin thoughtfully. Stella appeared in the office doorway. "You men up for some coffee this morning?" She needn't have asked twice.

We all sat around for the next hour sipping coffee and talking about families, cattle, and who was doing what to whom around the countryside. I'd have plenty of gossipy news to share with Blue Flower, Kate, and Sarah back at Rising Cross. Importantly though, Klappenbach was impressed that I reckoned to make another cattle drive up to the North Platte country in the Nebraska Territory.

We chatted with Klappenbach for the time it takes to enjoy three cups of Stella's coffee, long enough to give me a good sense of what we faced here in Bandera. I took a final swallow. I'd drunk enough to have to excuse myself to the privy out back.

As I emerged from the back door of Klappenbach's store, a shot rang out and a bullet splintered the doorjamb inches from my head. I dove back inside.

Hardy and Klappenbach came running at the sound.

I got on my belly and took a cautious peek outside. Off to my right, a few puffs of gun smoke lingered alongside a tree. Whomever had taken the shot didn't stick around. Warning? Bad aim? I finally stood.

"You okay, boss?" asked Hardy.

I nodded.

"Let me check it out," Hardy added, as he warily strode over to the spot beside the tree from which the erstwhile bushwhacker had taken his shot. He reached down and picked up a casing. He scanned the area. No one was in sight.

Meanwhile, I did make use of that privy. As I

emerged, Hardy was before me with bullet casing in hand.

"You'd a thought a bushwhacker would've used a rifle," he said with a scratch of his chin. "This is from a revolver, likely a Colt. Fella wasn't much of a shot." He handed the casing to me.

I shrugged. "It was too close to have been a warning, Hardy. Someone doesn't want us in Bandera." I looked over at Klappenbach.

"You boys best get your business done with Hoffman and mosey on out of Bandera," he said, as he examined the splintered wood in the doorjamb.

"Much obliged for your hospitality, August." I shook Klappenbach's hand and led Hardy around front to our horses. I looked about, but only the usual folks were to be seen walking the streets taking care of their mid-morning business. We walked the horses to the jail.

I looked around before knocking and letting myself and Hardy in. "You at home, Sheriff?" I asked as good-humored as possible.

"Coffee's over yonder," said Hoffman with a finger pointed to a blackened kettle setting on a small credenza. He leaned back in a beat-up old oak swivel chair behind an equally battered desk. He took a long pull on a foul-smelling cigar and blew a column of smoke skyward.

One whiff of the kettle contents dissuaded me from enjoying the sheriff's proffered hospitality. "Just drank enough at Klappenbach's to keep me awake all night, Sheriff," I offered as an excuse for snubbing his concoction.

"Have a seat," invited Hoffman with a wave toward a couple of chairs. "What's important enough for y'all to brave a trip to Bandera?"

I instinctively wiped the dust from the chair seat and

sat. Hoffman had enough offensive odors going on in the tiny space that comprised his office that I found myself disinclined to linger over conversation. "There was a murder and horse stealing at Rising Cross a couple of days ago. I lost a good hand in Brawny Jones."

The sheriff gave me a hard look. He wiped away a lingering piece of breakfast still stuck in his whiskers. "You know about a black stallion with white forelock that found its way to your spread?"

Hoffman's question took me totally by surprise. "I've seen the horse," I responded.

He must have read my face like a book. "Hoss belongs to that Rolf Schultz fella. Cayuse must've wandered out to your ranch, Mr. O'Toole. Surely, no one at Rising Cross would steal a man's horse." Hoffman flashed a smile loaded with contempt. "Now, I saw Mr. Schultz with his horse yesterday, so I guess it was returned to him. As to someone being shot, maybe your man was mistaken for a horse thief." Hoffman had his story all wrapped up in lies and tied in a pretty bow.

It was clear that I'd make no progress with the sheriff. "I guess my business here is done, Sheriff," I said and began to stand.

"Wait a second, Mr. O'Toole. Where were y'all last night?"

I can't say as I appreciated the accusatory tone of Hoffman's question. "We were about a half-day ride north of Bandera. Why do you ask, Sheriff?"

"That newspaperman Gordon Small was found dead in an alley last night. Figured he wrote some unkind news about you." The implication that I'd harm him for publishing lies about me was absurd.

"Now, I don't think that you—a man of faith—had

anything to do with it, Mr. O'Toole, but you surely understand my suspicion."

I got the impression that Hoffman was enjoying this. "Well, you're right that I wouldn't dream of harming that newspaperman, Sheriff. He posed no threat to me."

"You're treading a thin line here, Sheriff," contributed Hardy. "Do you have some sort of evidence?"

"Who are you to question what I have?" said Hoffman, swiveling his chair toward Hardy.

"As a former Texas Ranger, I do know a thing or two about due process, Sheriff. I'd say that you need to back off." Hardy gave the sheriff a don't-mess-with-me look. "If you're siding with that troublemaker Rolf Schultz, you might have bitten off a tad more than you can chew."

It was quite obvious from his body language that Hoffman didn't appreciate the threat. He decided not to push the newspaperman killing any further. The sheriff found himself between a rock and a hard place, as he found himself dealing with the strong emotions rampaging through the countryside. "Sometimes, you gotta go along to get along," he finally spat out. He'd finally revealed himself as the spineless creature that he had repeatedly shown himself to be. He was all about protecting his own skin.

I nodded to Hardy. "We'll see no justice here. Let's go," I said firmly and headed for the door.

"Y'all think twice about coming back here," said Hoffman as a parting warning. "I don't have enough men to protect y'all."

EIGHT
FINDING ESCAPED SLAVES

AS HARDY and I wended our way northward from Bandera, we couldn't help but lament the goings on in the town. Folks still fretted about Indians, of course, but the issues surrounding slavery and the accompanying emotional turmoil had now far-exceeded the worry over attacks by hostiles.

I'd heard that the McGregors had set up his black-smith shop in Fredericksburg and wondered whether he still had connections to folks helping slaves escape bondage. "Reckon to ride up to Fredericksburg in a couple of days, Hardy."

"Yuh got business up thataway, boss?" responded Hardy.

"I expect to," I responded. Fredericksburg was a long way from the farms that benefited from slave labor. The vast majority of the hundred and eighty thousand slaves in Texas were in the eastern part of our state. With my rapidly increasing land holdings came an ever-greater influence, but I was as yet not in a position to exercise it. Men twice my age held the purse strings of the government and wielded the power in Austin. Despite my increasing reputation as a rancher and trail boss among cattleman circles, the politicians wed to slave labor brushed me off as a young whippersnapper who hadn't yet earned a place among their elite number.

"Need more drovers?" asked Hardy. He knew what I was looking to do.

"Worked out well last time. Folks freed from bondage don't know how to live a normal life, Hardy. Cowboying gives them a skill set to survive as free men." George Freeman had told me of stories he'd heard of escaped slaves returning to bondage because they didn't know how to live as free men. Having escaped slavery himself, I reckoned George knew what he was talking about. It made perfect sense to me.

"Gotta admire what yer doin', boss."

"It's not getting caught doing it that makes it difficult. We've seen firsthand the vigilantism that folks can be stirred up to do. And that was based on simple rumor."

"What do yuh make of that newspaper fella Small bein' killed?" Hardy was genuinely curious.

"He sure stirred folks up with his writing," I responded. I hadn't yet given much thought to what sort of motive resulted in Small's murder.

"Maybe he was gonna write somethin' Schultz didn't cotton none to," suggested Hardy.

I hadn't considered that. Most of the violence appeared to be committed by pro-slavery folks, and Small's killing had the earmarks of something Schultz might conjure up. Then again, why would he eliminate his mouthpiece? This slavery business was growing uglier every day.

Plodding along and keeping an eye out for trouble, we

discussed the upcoming trail drive now and again until we finally came within view of Rising Cross Ranch. As we approached, the lanterns inside the main house and bunkhouse gave off a warm, welcoming glow. We took care of our horses and went our separate ways, Hardy to the bunkhouse and me to Blue Flower's waiting arms. I figured to spend a couple of days reacquainting myself with my wife and young sons before heading to Fredericksburg.

————

I'D LEARNED that Sam Houston's term representing Texas in the US Senate had ended, and he was seeking to once again be governor. From the occasional newspaper that came our way, I observed that he tended to be against radical political leanings. He'd even voted against the Compromise of 1850. Though he owned slaves, he'd voted against the Kansas-Nebraska Act that he saw as increasing tensions over slavery. It had caused him to leave the Democratic Party. Even though I paid little attention because I couldn't vote, Houston even ran for president in 1856. It all left me wondering how his outsized presence as the preeminent Texan would sway pro-slavery forces in Texas. I hoped I'd get to meet him, just as I'd met and might have influenced Governor Runnels. I hoped Will McGregor might have some insights, assuming the pro-slavery folks hadn't chased him off again.

"I'm heading out to Fredericksburg tomorrow," I said to Blue Flower over breakfast. She was getting used to my being away for long periods. It was a blessing that we were surrounded by family and friends here at Rising Cross Ranch, so she never had cause to feel lonely at my absences. While my time at home was filled with ranching chores, the loving attention I devoted to her and our boys tended to compensate.

"You see McGregor?" she asked.

"I'm hoping he can help me find a couple of escaped slaves that we can teach to drive cattle."

Blue Flower nodded. "Is good what you do," she said with pride as she nursed baby Peter. George and Isa ran about the house, making more noise than a stirred-up gaggle of geese.

My mission to help slaves to freedom would surely have been doomed without her support. "I figure to take Shorty and Buck with me," I offered. I especially wanted Shorty along, as he'd have to pay special attention to the slaves we trained to drove cattle.

"Kate thinks you should take Will," she offered.

"Is she…"

Blue Flower nodded. "She with child again."

Apparently, Kate needed a bit of time to herself. I laughed. "Okay. I'll take Will along instead of Buck." I didn't want to pull all the men from the ranch, as cows were calving and horses foaling. Hardy, Buck, and Isaac were enough to handle chores for a few days. "Expect I'll be gone about five days," I added. That was a clue as to how much food to pack.

Blue Flower smiled and ran her tongue slowly over her lips.

It was her signal that she'd include sweet bear sign in among the jerky, biscuits, and pemmican.

———

SHORTY, Will, and I headed out at break of dawn. As we headed to Fredericksburg, it occurred to me that we were only a couple of weeks from my planned rendezvous with Spirit Talker at the intersection of the Pinta Trail and Pedernales River, not far from Fredericksburg. The ride to Fredericksburg took us the better part of two days. We had pushed hard but spared the horses by alternately walking and riding. I'd toyed with bringing a packhorse but decided not to, as we'd be more mobile and less attractive to bandits or hostile Kiowa or Comanche.

We rode single file along the mostly narrow trail, so there was little conversation. Shorty and Will were well aware of what I was up to.

Late afternoon of the second day, we reined in in front of what appeared to be a thriving smithy shop. I noted that there was no church attached to it—yet. McGregor had brought his sign with him from Austin. It was a tad shopworn, but there it was for all the world to see:

WILLIAM MCGREGOR
Smithy and Preacher
Sins & Iron Hammered Out Here

There would be no doubt to anyone as to Will McGregor's mission in life. Behind the smithy shop was a roomy lean-to-like structure fashioned of logs and sod. We hitched our horses out front. I'd barely taken a step toward the shop when a gentle voice stopped me.

"Why Jack O'Toole! I do declare!" It was McGregor's wife, Colleen. "Welcome to Fredericksburg."

"Colleen, these are my hands, Shorty and Will. Reckoned I owed y'all a visit. Is Will around?"

"Y'all arrived just in time for dinner. It'll take but a few minutes to whip up a bit more. Come on back to our humble abode," she said with a warm smile. She was about to lead the way but paused. "There's a small corral out back. By the time you've tended your horses, I'll have piping hot stew on the table." She paused. "We're so glad to see y'all."

It didn't take long to tend our cayuses. Big Red welcomed a break from the heavier-than-usual load. As we turned to enter the McGregor's home, Will McGregor appeared. He gave me a bear hug and obliged Shorty and Will with the same warm welcome. He turned to me. "So good tuh see yuh, lad." He still spoke with a heavy brogue. "How's the family?"

"Family is fine, Will."

We were soon seated around a small but adequate table, enjoying Colleen's beef stew. "So, what's brung yuh lads to Fredericksburg?" asked McGregor.

"We're going to drive more beeves north. I figured to train a couple more escaped slaves as drovers. My hope is that you might still have connections to get us maybe three or four Black men." My request was direct. There was no point in pulling any punches.

The McGregors exchanged glances. Widow Jenks among others had paid with their lives to help slaves escape. With Runnels leaving office and Rip Ford chasing bandits to the south, Will McGregor's connections to the politically powerful appeared to have dwindled. His response confirmed my fears. "I'm not sure we can help yuh, lad," McGregor said ruefully.

I took my first sip of coffee, and it set me back. The brew was so strong, it likely caused my chest hair to grow another inch. My reaction seemed to ease the tension generated by McGregor's discouraging news.

"It's not all that bad, Jack," soothed Colleen. She turned to her husband. "Tell him, Will."

I gave McGregor a questioning gaze.

"There are powerful forces at work, Jack. They play upon folks' fears. I fear there's tyranny afoot and our nation's barely eighty years old." He looked off thoughtfully. "Fear. Fear comes in many shapes. Fear plantation owners won't be able to meet the demand for cotton. Fear that after taking away slaves, the government will take away other things dear to us. Fear of violence. Fear of a rebellion of slaves. But always fear," lamented McGregor.

Shorty's and Will's forkfuls of breakfast were frozen in midair, as they listened intently to his wise words. "Sounds like an uphill battle," offered Shorty.

"Aye, that it is," responded McGregor.

Colleen gave her husband one of those *wife* looks that says *get to the point*.

McGregor turned to me. "But this isn't helpin' yuh, lad." He stuffed a forkful of eggs into his mouth and wiped a dribble from his ample red beard. "There's a fella over toward Austin that might help. Name's Cutter Kincaid. Pretty much a vagabond, but if yer timin' be right, he'd be a help." McGregor chuckled. "He lives underground. He has a heart fer slaves."

"Underground?" I echoed.

The McGregors both nodded. "Makes sense, though. He dug out a cave to protect himself from Indians," said McGregor. "I'll give yuh directions best I can, lad."

"We appreciate your help," I replied.

"This the only reason yuh come to Fredericksburg? Couldn't have been just to see us."

"I do need to see the sheriff," I confessed. "Have some personal effects from three victims of an Apache attack a couple of months back."

"Three, you say?"

"Yes. We found them badly cut and tied spread-eagle-like for the buzzards. They'd been hunting at the wrong time and place."

"Bet they were the Barton brothers," mused McGregor. "Their family's been lookin' for them. Went out hunting and never returned."

"One named Sam?" I queried.

"Matter of fact, yes," responded McGregor.

"Good to know. The family can have closure, some peace of mind," I suggested.

We finished breakfast and drained the coffee pot while McGregor drew us a crude map to Cutter Kincaid's erstwhile abode. We thanked them and bade farewell. I admit to having been anxious to get home and try to find the man McGregor told us about.

We dropped the Barton brothers' personal effects with the sheriff, telling him the nature of their violent demise. He wrote up a report. We were about to mount up and head out of Fredericksburg, when I brought myself up short.

"What's on yer mind, boss?" asked Shorty.

"Nearly forgot to drop in on our old friend Reggie Wilson," I said with a smile. I tried to envision him in his city-slicker suit and the bowler perched on his head.

I looked up the street, and there it was: *Wilson's Mercantile*. We walked our horses the short distance, hitched them, and entered the store.

Reggie was standing with his back to the front door as he placed merchandise on some shelves. "Welcome, let me know if I can help," he intoned.

"Is that any way to treat friends?" I teased.

At the sound of my voice, Reggie spun around. A broad smile graced his face. "Great to see you," he responded. "Care for some coffee?" He'd learned the way to visitors' hearts here on the frontier.

"Thanks. Just had some up at the McGregor's place. We're headed out, but didn't want to miss seeing you." I took a scan of the store. "Looks as though you're doing well, Reggie."

"Spending time at Rising Cross helped, Mr. O'Toole. I'm able to maintain a stock of the supplies folks truly need." He grew serious. "We heard about Brawny. Sorry. The world's going crazy."

"Thanks kindly. We have an idea who was responsible, but the sheriff in Bandera is no help."

"Not sure the sheriff here would be much help either."

I gave a tight smile. "The law has pretty much caved to politics. I fear it'll get worse. Fredericksburg is likely a decent place to be if bigger trouble starts, Reggie. These German immigrants are strong and mostly don't like slavery so may steer clear of any violence."

"I appreciate the advice, Mr. O'Toole," responded Reggie.

A sunbonnet caught my eye. I pointed to it. "Wrap that up for Will here to give to Kate."

Will gave me a bashful look.

"You must keep your woman happy, Will." I turned back to Reggie. "Matter of fact, wrap that other one, the one with the blue ribbon and flower." I looked at Shorty.

"Don't look at me, boss. I got no woman an' ain't wearin' that thing." His laugh broke any tension.

We departed Wilson's Mercantile with our merchandise and headed from Fredericksburg.

As we rode along the south bank of the Pedernales River, Shorty came alongside. "What's next, boss?"

"I'm thinking of sending Will back to Rising Cross while you and I find this Cutter Kincaid fellow."

Will overheard and gave me a look that said he yearned to stay with us.

"Somebody must let Blue Flower know what we're up to, Will. I need Shorty with me, because he'll be ramrodding the trail drive. It's important that he feels comfortable with any escaped slaves we find. Besides, Kate will be missing you about now." I chuckled best I could. I didn't know whether my sister was ready for his return. Sometimes, women could be hard to figure. The sunbonnet would help. "I'll be hanging back from this trail drive, Will. Shorty will need you, Hardy, Perez, and Buck."

The prospect of the trail drive seemed to resonate with Will, much to my relief. I didn't need an unhappy pouting cowboy on my hands, brother-in-law or not.

We rode to the intersection of the Pedernales River and the Pinta Trail. Will turned southward while we continued along the river with hopes of finding Cutter Kincaid's cave north of Austin.

———

MOSTLY FLAT AND decidedly rugged were the best words to describe the landscape north of the Texas capital. The land swept away from what was called the Balcones Escarpment, a long cliff-like ridge that ran hundreds of miles from the southwest to northeast across Central Texas. Land to its east was mostly the territory of slave trade and labor.

Shorty and I did our best to follow McGregor's crude map. There weren't many landmarks save for the rivers. The Pedernales eventually joined the Colorado River which we crossed and turned northward. I was intent on keeping us clear of Austin proper, as I wasn't prepared to get involved with the powerful folks that ran the government.

We'd been traveling for three days since Will departed. Every arroyo, every hill, every creek looked the same. "Wonder whether there's anyone around who know him, boss?" asked Shorty impatiently.

I was on the verge of giving up, when we made a turn up an arroyo and a deep bass voice boomed out seemingly from nowhere.

"Whatcha be lookin' fer?"

"Cutter Kincaid?" I responded tentatively.

"Who be lookin'?" inquired the voice.

"Jack O'Toole and Shorty McBride. Will McGregor sent us."

There was a rustling sound from the tall grasses and brush. "I be Cutter Kincaid." The human that stood before us was a sight to behold. He couldn't have been more than five feet tall. He wore a pointy cock-eyed hat with a wide brim over a face featuring a long, scraggy beard. His boots climbed nearly to the knees of his bowed legs, and he bore a belly that hung prodigiously over his belt. Two things especially drew my special attention. One was the Colt Navy revolver holstered on his hip. The other was a bejeweled silver cross dangling from a chain around his scruffy neck. "You huntin', sellin', or buyin'?—Slaves, that is?" He gave me a hard look then burst out with a laugh.

I was relieved that this apparition had a sense of humor, bizarre as it seemed. "Freein'," I responded with a confident smile.

"McGregor, eh?" he mused. "Whatcha figger to do with slaves?"

"I train them to be drovers on my trail drives—sort of an underground railroad north to freedom."

"That dog—he looks more like a wolf," he pointed to Zeb.

"He is a wolf," I responded. I decided to not explain. Zeb was obviously not a typical wolf that might have been at Cutter Kincaid's throat.

Cutter Kincaid nodded but kept an eye on Zeb. He finally laid a gracious but toothless smile upon us. "You boys camp right here tonight. Don't be leavin' til I get back." With that, he disappeared.

Shorty and I shook our heads. "Where'd that elf go?" asked Shorty.

I shrugged and began unloading Big Red.

"You trust him?" persisted Shorty.

"Don't have much choice. Still, we'll keep our eyes open." Soon enough, we were both bedded down among the grasses and fast asleep.

———

IF THE SUN hadn't wakened us, the jangling of chains would have. We heard them before we saw them, and I rubbed the sleep from my eyes as fast as I could. Cutter Kincaid appeared with three fine specimens of manhood. Two of the Black men wore manacles with chains.

We quickly learned how he'd gotten the name *Cutter*, as he produced a massive set of shears from his cave-like hovel. He made short work of the remaining manacles.

"Figger dogs will be along in a couple of hours. Better git."

"What about you?" I asked.

He produced a glass jar and screwed off the lid. It was the foulest smelling concoction that ever wafted across our noses. "Dogs don't like this. Mess up them sniffers fer weeks." He gave a broad grin. Skunks smelled sweet by comparison.

I slipped my hand in a pocket and began to pull out a sack of coin.

Cutter Kincaid raised a hand to stop me. "No need, son. Just git these men to freedom."

"Much obliged," I said in parting. We had a lot of walking ahead of us to put distance between us and the possibility of slave catchers with vicious manhunting dogs. Also, we didn't have enough food for five men. I wished I'd brought my bow and arrows, as I was quite reluctant to bring any unwanted attention to us. If we came upon game, I'd have to chance a rifle shot. Meanwhile, I hoped none of the slaves were hungry.

I asked no questions of Cutter Kincaid. I didn't really have the time. How had he come up with three escaped slaves in a matter of a few hours? Where were they from? Who had they escaped from? Were they house slaves or field slaves? Questions lingered. Immediacy trumped curiosity.

Unlike the last time we escorted escaped slaves to Rising Cross Ranch, we had neither a slaver wagon nor forged bills of sale. We'd concentrate on our escape and get acquainted later. I didn't even know whether these Blacks were literate.

NINE
ON THE RUN

AFTER THREE HOURS of walking in the baking hot sun, it was a relief to find a shady spot to make camp. We'd finally be able to begin to get acquainted with our Black companions. By now, we'd managed to learn their names or at least the ones given them by their owners: James, Frederick, and Paul. We also learned that they'd all been field hands. That may have accounted for the ease in which Cutter Kincaid had found and freed them.

The Black men seemed extraordinarily nervous. I could hardly blame them given the circumstances. I began getting acquainted while Shorty set up camp. Between the hot weather and our need for stealth, we decided against a campfire. We still had a meager supply of beef jerky and pemmican, so cooking was unnecessary. Yes, hot coffee would be missed.

The Black men sat side-by-side cross-legged under the spreading branches of a large live oak. I sat myself down opposite them. Zeb lay beside me, his great head resting in his forepaws. The expressions of the Black men might be best described as apprehensive at the sight of a great wolf. I placed my hand on Zeb's forehead, and that seemed to put the men at ease. I assumed they all understood English. "James," I opened my inquiry to the tallest of the three. "Tell me about yourself."

His dolefully forlorn expression said plenty. "Where go?" he asked.

"I'm taking you to a place where you'll be free." I smiled as warmly as I could muster.

"I free at home," he responded. He looked hard at me. "What you call free?"

The other two escaped slaves nodded agreement with James's question.

"Free to make your own choices," I replied. "To help you be free, I must know you better."

James nodded. "I pick cotton and fix sheds for master. Live here many years."

"Do you have a family?" I asked.

James shook his head. "Had woman. Master call her breeder. Sell her."

I shook my head. I'd heard similar tales from others.

Frederick chimed in. "No woman. Work hard," he said while staring into the ground. I had a sense that he wasn't being straight with me.

The slave named Paul remained silent.

I shrugged and reckoned to get some sort of conversation underway. "My name is Jack O'Toole, and this man is Shorty McGuire. I own a ranch two days west of here. I drive cattle north to sell. Last year, we taught three escaped slaves much like yourselves how to work cattle. They helped with the trail drive. When we reached our destination, they were free. They decided to raise their own cattle and horses."

"Where are they?" asked Frederick.

"They decided to stay in Nebraska Territory on the

North Platte River. They own a ranch. It is a beautiful place."

About this time, Paul looked up. He had strikingly beautiful eyes and full lips. With slender fingers, he pulled off his thick cloth headscarf, and a mass of hair tumbled to his shoulders.

"Holy smoke!" exclaimed Shorty at the sight.

"Why, you're a woman!" I said with surprise.

"Sheesha," said the Black woman, pointing to herself. She blinked her dark eyes and finally smiled at having finally revealed herself.

I looked questioningly at James and Frederick. They shrugged. Caught off guard, I needed a moment to gather my thoughts. A new dynamic had been created. I looked skyward as though asking God what He was doing to me?

James seemed to sense my discomfort. He threw a question at me. "What is free?"

I had never really gotten around to defining freedom for myself, much less anyone else. I suppose I had a vague idea that it had to do with being free to make our own choices about life. I recalled that God had bestowed free will upon mankind. Yet freedom wasn't so simple, as one man's freedom may not be so free to another. My Pa told me that our nation's Constitution enshrined our freedoms, and yet I knew that freedom was far greater than that given us by any government. My eyes went from one escaped slave to the other. They surely caught the deep seriousness revealed in my face.

I looked over at Shorty, but his body language said he'd be no help.

I took a deep breath. "Freedom is folks' right to choosing how and where they live so long as it doesn't prevent the freedom of others." I thought on that a second, especially upon seeing the quizzical expressions on James, Frederick, and Sheesha. "It can be a feeling, too. When I ride upon the far reaches of my ranch under a sky that seems to stretch forever or journey among the rushing rivers and majestic mountains of the north, I feel free. Knowing that I'm not held in bondage by any man is freedom."

Sheesha smiled and nodded her understanding. "Many slaves here," she observed.

"And many folks believe that is wrong. I'm one of them. Our Constitution states that we are free to speak, worship, and think as we please. It is immoral to be enslaved."

"Master think me breeder," Sheesha shared. Then she proceeded to slide closer to Frederick. "Frederick, my man."

We were making progress.

"Where we go? asked James.

"My home, it's called Rising Cross Ranch."

"What we do there? Will we be free?" James was full of questions.

"You are free to leave any time. You might not get very far because of the slave catchers and their dogs. But you are free to do as you choose." I let that sink in a moment. "Can any of you ride a horse or shoot a gun?"

"I ride horse," piped up Frederick. "Massa no let us shoot guns."

The others nodded.

"Are you willing to learn how to be cowboys, to ride horses, throw lassos, shoot guns, herd cattle?" I'd thrown them a load of skills that barely scratched the surface of what they'd need to learn. "You'll be fed and clothed. There will be other cowboys. We will be driving cattle northward to the Nebraska Territory."

"We are free?" asked Frederick, seeking assurance.

"You are always free to leave or stay."

"Why guns?" asked Sheesha.

"Bad people might attack us. Some will want to take you back to slavery. Others may want to steal our cattle or horses. We must defend ourselves." My answer was about as straightforward as I could make it.

Shorty began handing out jerky and pemmican. "I'm what is called the trail boss. Y'all will work fer me until we get to Nebraska. We have a friend there that will help you, if you decide to stay."

"Who friend?" asked James.

"George Freeman. He escaped slavery in Mississippi, was helped by Pawnee Indians, married an Indian woman, learned to be a cowboy, and now owns a ranch on the North Platte River where we're headed," said Shorty, friendly-like.

"He free?" asked Sheesha.

"Very free," I replied.

"Looks like a clear night, boss," noted Shorty. "With a half moon and plenty of stars, it might make sense to be traveling."

I looked at our three companions. "Y'all up to more walking?" I could see that they were tired.

"We pray to be strong," said Frederick.

It was the first hint among them of religious faith. "God gives us strength," I responded. I felt a tad ashamed that I'd failed to ask them. I suppose I took others' faith in God for granted. My response brought reassuring smiles. The sharing of our faith introduced an element of trust. We were soon walking westward.

Shorty walked beside me. "That went well, boss," he shared in a near whisper.

I nodded. "We've got a lot of work ahead," I

observed. "The drive can't wait past the end of May. I wonder whether Sheesha can handle cowboying."

Shorty chuckled. "Guess it'll be cowgirling, boss."

"We'll let her decide. Maybe she'd rather help Perez with cooking." I let that sink in. Sheesha was free to choose so long as she contributed skills to support the trail drive. "Keep your eyes peeled for rattlers, javelinas, and slave catchers, Shorty." I figured it didn't hurt to remind us that we were a long way from the safety of home.

TEN
HEAD 'EM NORTH

WE MANAGED to come within spitting distance of Rising Cross Ranch with no notable incidents. We did dispose of a couple of rattlesnakes and fended off coyotes a time or two. The long walk allowed Shorty and me to get better acquainted with our companions. We strove to put into practice biblical principles like kindness, compassion, humility, gentleness, and patience.

Sheesha took me aside as we drew near the ranch buildings. "Sheesha learn to be cowboy," she confided. She stole a glance at Frederick who nodded reluctant approval.

I shook my head incredulously. She wasn't going to be trapped in someone else's idea of the roles women should play in life. Importantly, Sheesha had grasped what freedom meant. She was hardly any bigger than my young brother Buck. I tried to imagine her wrangling a fifteen-hundred-pound longhorn but said nothing. "You'll have to earn it," I advised.

Sheesha smiled confidently.

Upon consideration, she was sure tough enough to

have risked escape from a life of bondage. It remained to be seen whether she'd be up to the rigors of the cowboy life.

I looked forward to being back in Blue Flower's loving arms. It seemed that I was surrounded by tough women. Guess they had to be pretty resilient to survive in what was decidedly a man's world.

I left the three Black folks to Shorty. I reckoned to let him figure how to deal with a woman in the bunkhouse. The very thought triggered a chuckle.

———

THUS FAR, no one had come to welcome us home. It was right hot, one of those days when everything that figured to survive sought shade. I reflected on the journey across the mostly flat terrain since we'd departed Cutter Kincaid's place. It had been growing warmer, but there were enough breezes to take the edge off the heat. Here at Rising Cross, the heat just seemed to sit unmoving and stifling. As if on cue, a trickle of sweat found its way down my back. The bandanna around my neck was soaking wet, though that had a cooling effect. The windows of the house were open wide as an invitation to any breeze that happened by. I quietly strode through the open door with Zeb trotting behind me.

Blue Flower sat on the relatively cool floor playing with George and Isa while nursing Peter. She looked up with that beautiful smile of hers. "Pohya Isa home," she said softly.

I was about to hang my hat, when I remembered that it made a decent fan. I leaned over and gave her a kiss while tousling the hair of twins George and Isa.

I glanced over at the dining table. A weathered envelope was conspicuous by its presence at the place I normally sat. We rarely got mail out here. I looked over at Blue Flower.

"Was on gallery. No see who leave," she said. She got up and padded to our bedroom to put Peter in his crib for a nap. She returned as I poured myself a cup of coffee.

I hadn't yet touched the envelope. I sat staring at it.

Blue Flower looked curiously at me. "Open?" she queried.

I sighed. Mysterious envelopes with no markings identifying the sender was a tad concerning. Someone didn't want their identity known. I slipped out my Bowie knife. It was pretty much overkill for the task at hand, but it was sharp and easily slit open the envelope. I gently shook the envelope and a notebook fell from it onto the table. A notebook?

"What is?" asked Blue Flower.

I flipped through the pages. My jaw gaped. These were Gordon Small's notes! "These are the notes from the newspaperman that wrote lies about me." I placed the notebook on the table and stared at it. I suppose I was in a sort of state of shock. Who had sent the notebook? Why?

"What it say?" pressed Blue Flower.

My mind finally came around to the here and now. Could it be that something in the notebook led to Small's murder? Was someone providing me with evidence? I thumbed through the pages. The notes were brief. Small also used a sort of shorthand that made reading challenging. The first several pages were notes about wagon trains and frontier life. About halfway through, his writings turned to slavery. He'd apparently connected with Rolf Schultz, and his subsequent notes were decidedly pro-slavery. I found the section about me and Small's sharing Schultz's promotion of me as an abolitionist who needed silencing. The final half dozen pages read like an exposé of Schultz's methods. Schultz received financial support and orders from a wealthy plantation owner in Mississippi named Byron Lee. As I read, it became ever-clearer that Small intended to write a newspaper piece exposing Schultz. If Shultz knew what Small was up to, it was enough motivation to kill the newspaper reporter. It sure changed my opinion of Small. Yes, his columns had caused me considerable trouble, including nearly getting lynched, but he'd figured Schultz out and was about to make things right. "The notes say that Small was going to expose Rolf Schultz, the man who tried to kill me and likely killed Brawny."

"You still must meet Mukwooru," Blue Flower reminded me.

I nodded and thoughtfully turned the notebook over and over in my hands, but my mind was racing. What would Sheriff Hoffman do with this evidence? I decided the truth I held in my hands still wasn't enough to turn Hoffman to recognize Schultz as the evildoer he was. I finally stood and laid the notebook beside my rifle on the fireplace mantle. "I meet Mukwooru in two weeks," I assured Blue Flower. My Comanche brother Spirit Talker and I might be able to come up with a way to entrap Schultz. Our minds did tend to enjoy the hunt, and this prey would be a worthy prize. Meanwhile, we would have our hands full converting three field hands into drovers. We'd be doing exceptionally well to instill the basics.

———

SHORTY, Will, Hardy, and Buck worked doubly hard to teach the escaped slaves the rudiments of cowboying. After plenty of tumbles from saddles, the trio learned to ride. Handling guns was another matter. None of them were up to hitting a barn at close range. Sheesha actually picked up the lasso faster than James and Frederick.

I strolled out to the barn one morning about a week before the trail drive was scheduled to depart. I figured to give Big Red a bit of exercise and came upon Frederick and Sheesha kissing. "Is this how y'all muck stalls?" I asked nonchalantly.

Despite their dark skin, I sensed deep blushes.

"Y'all might think about what the good Lord might find right in His eyes." I gave Frederick a seriously hard look. "Hold your feelings off until after the trail drive, Frederick. The trail between here and the North Platte is long and very rough. It won't be a place for this sort of distraction. Am I understood? What y'all do at the end of the drive is up to you." I smiled, but they could see that I was deadly serious.

The two nodded and grabbed shovels to resume mucking the barn stalls.

I made a mental note to remind Shorty to keep an eye on the two.

———

BLUE FLOWER and I watched the dust disappear in the distance, as Shorty led the drive northward in a cloud of dust. We'd pulled together a decidedly modest herd of just over four hundred beeves. About a hundred were from Sam Collions's Circle C Ranch. The bellowing of longhorns and neighing of horses faded before the dust cloud left in their wake. It would be a good test for

Shorty and leave me here with the opportunity to team with Spirit Talker to expose Rolf Schultz for the paid troublemaker and likely murderer that he was. It was time for justice to prevail, even in the face of the passions inflaming the entire frontier. Revealing Schultz would be an antidote of sorts to the spreading poison that was slavery.

ELEVEN
A HUNT

THERE WERE no clouds to be seen, as I sat comfortably under a live oak near the south bank of the Pedernales River where the Pinta Trail crossed. Describing the Pedernales as a river was a bit of an overstatement. There was very little water flowing. Flowing? That was also an overstatement. Water meandered reluctantly from one pool to another. Anyone crossing need not worry about being able to swim. Shucks, it could be done with not so much as a drop of water on your boots.

I watched the sun hang, casting its pinkish-orange glow just above the western horizon. The Nebraska Territory had its majestic lofty mountain peaks and rushing waters, but my soul was wed to Texas. The sky seemed to stretch forever and beyond. God sure was good. I hoped and prayed that Shorty had met with no difficulties, as he negotiated the Texas Panhandle. The moon would be full this night, but Spirit Talker had yet to appear.

My small campfire was beginning to die and drowsiness was overtaking me, when the snap of a twig brought me to full attention.

"*Aitu!*"

The Comanche word for something not good served to relax me.

Spirit Talker emerged from the gathering darkness. "I almost surprise Pohya Isa." He lamented.

"Welcome to my campfire Mukwooru," I said with an inviting smile and hugged my Comanche brother. "You had me worried."

Spirit Talker laughed.

"*Ana o'a hi'it.*" I responded with an invite to enjoy a piece of rabbit meat. It was quite lean but fine for my hungry guest.

I stirred the fire, and we sat for a few moments making small talk about family while Spirit Talker savored the rabbit.

"You no go on trail drive?" Spirit Talker asked.

I shook my head.

He gave me a nod, as though reading my expression that I had some concern.

"A man named Rolf Schultz is stirring up trouble. I think he's killed a couple of people and tried to have me lynched."

"Lynched?" Spirit Talker asked curiously.

I made a choking motion with my hand around my neck. "Brawny saved my life." I held off a tear at the memory. "Schultz or one of his men killed Brawny."

Spirit Talker shook his head. "Men evil."

"I'm doubtful that Sheriff Hoffman will be much help, but it's time for justice." I hunkered down toward the campfire and poked it with a stick. "I don't want to take the law into my own hands."

Spirit Talker nodded, then offered a devious smile. "We set trap?" he said more as a statement than question.

I smiled. "Yep. A little *kaahaniitu* should work." We'd deceive Schultz and lead him into a trap. It would be too easy to bushwhack the man on one of his regular journeys to Fredericksburg, but I wasn't up to murdering him no matter how evil his deeds. Then again, if the law wouldn't put a stop to him, did I have a choice?

"What God do?" asked Spirit Talker.

At this moment, I really didn't need a lesson in morality much less God's will. I looked up to the heavens then back at the fire. "Any ideas?" I sighed.

"Maybe scare *tosa* away?" suggested Spirit Talker.

"Scare him?" I asked curiously.

Spirit Talker picked up a stick and sketched a rudimentary map of the trail from Bandera to Fredericksburg in the dirt alongside the campfire. "Take three days. Two nights dark. Many things can happen," he said, pointing first at Bandera and then Schultz's destination. He proceeded to draw *Xs* at two places along the trail where Schultz would likely camp. I recognized them as affording good cover. Spirit Talker motioned at Zeb. "Isa be part of plan."

"We're going to scare him to death," I stated flatly.

"We hunt. See what happen."

The hunt began.

———

WE TRAVELED down the Pinta Trail toward Bandera. At some point, we reckoned that our path would intersect with Schultz's. Patience was especially critical on this hunt. Unlike most animal prey that tended to be instinctive, humans had the capacity to think and therefore be less predictable. We had to be ready for most anything.

Well, *anything* happened. We were walking our horses

southward in parallel to the Pinta Trail, when we heard horses approaching. We were well-hidden, and our cayuses knew to be quiet. I could barely hear Zeb's pants in the dry summer heat.

It was Schultz, all right. But he wasn't alone. Two heavily armed riders accompanied him. The two looked like downright nasty customers. They rode single file with Schultz between them.

Spirit Talker looked at me and gave a decidedly devious smile. We were at a place off the trail on high ground where any pursuit by an enemy would be impossible, yet we had a full view of Schultz's little band. He drew an arrow from his quiver and motioned me to do the same. "No *peeka*," he whispered. We would not shoot to kill. "Shoot, yell, run," he said, delighting in his trickery.

We shot our arrows at the same time and hollered war whoops. The arrows narrowly missed the lead rider and stuck in a close-by tree in plain sight. The rider dove from his saddle, revolver in hand. Schultz's horse reared, while the escort behind him also dove for cover. All they could hear in the immediate silence after our feigned attack was our horses galloping away.

We rode perhaps a half mile before pulling up. I couldn't suppress a grin.

"They *kuya akatu*."

Indeed, they had a bit of *kuya akatu*—fear—instilled in them. It occurred to me that repeating the fake attack wouldn't be so effective. We would have to raise the stakes, so to speak. I figured that we actually might scare off Schultz's escort. As though on cue, Zeb appeared with his pack. I looked to the heavens. "What are you telling me, Lord?"

Spirit Talker's amazement was writ large across his

face. Walks With Wolves still delivered powerful *sunipu*. It was Godly medicine not to be trifled with.

Thus, Zeb would have a key role in our next harassing attack on Schultz and his escorts. I wrung my hands with delight. Hopefully, my confidence wasn't premature. We rode at a quicker pace for about three miles to get well ahead of Schultz. We had in mind a place near where the Pinta Trail and Guadalupe River intersected. There was a ridge offering a high vantage point overlooking the trail from which we could stage our deception and again escape easily. The sun was creeping inexorably toward its meeting with the horizon. Schultz would likely camp beneath the bluff. Our next endeavor would work best in the dim light of early evening.

Zeb was joined by his pack. Our plan was to have the wolves appear along the top of the ridge. Combined with Comanche incantations, a couple of well-placed arrows, and a special surprise, we expected that our attack would be going up a notch in terms of its impact.

It didn't take long for the trio to appear. They looked about guardedly while looking for a spot to camp for the night. They talked among themselves, but I was unable to make out what they were saying. I had the impression that one of Schultz's escorts was of a mind to quit.

Spirit Talker's chanting carried in the early evening air. The three travelers looked about furtively with a mix of fear and curiosity. I sent an arrow into a tree behind them.

"Good Lord, Rolf! It's them Injuns agin'!" shouted one of the escorts.

At that, I delivered a long howl. Zeb and his pack of a half dozen lobos appeared above Schultz. Their bared teeth and penetrating eyes must have thrown fear of the wrath of God into the trio.

I shifted my howl to a war whoop and fired another arrow that stuck in a tree limb beside Schultz's head.

The three spurred their horses ahead. In the darkness, they couldn't see the trip line but felt the branch sweep them from their saddles. They hollered a bit and one landed on a cactus, but soon settled down, realizing that there was total silence. The wolves were gone, and I had deftly retrieved the arrows. Scared half to death, Schultz's two escorts scrambled for their horses, remounted and lit their way down the trail back toward Bandera. Schultz was left embarrassingly alone, sitting under a live oak tree with a huge tear in his trousers.

"Who's out there?" he called fearfully.

"*Peeka tabu, peeka tabu,*" called out Spirit Talker in as haunting a voice as he could muster.

"Kill coward, kill coward," I translated in an equally scary voice aimed at instilling abject fear in Schultz. I shot an arrow that stuck in the tree trunk just above his head.

"Wh...what do you want?" cried Schultz.

All was silent. I reckoned that by this time Schultz was totally perplexed. He was certainly filled with fear, fear of whatever unknown attacker had waylaid him.

Meanwhile, Spirit Talker, me, and the wolves had headed up the trail far enough to observe. I figured Schultz was full of himself enough to overcome his fear and resume his travel up the Pinta Trail. He'd be arrogant enough to figure that he didn't need the two who'd deserted him. Hopefully, our words about killing the coward weighed upon him. Most everyone feared death, not so much death itself as not knowing when or where.

Now that we outnumbered our prey, we could more readily choose the time and place to finish the hunt.

———

WE WATCHED SCHULTZ AWAKEN, as shards of sunlight stabbed his face. He'd fallen asleep sitting against the tree, exactly where we'd left him the night before. He glanced around as though wondering whether he'd had a bad dream. "Carl? Howard?" He called for the men that had deserted him. As he stood, his head brushed against the arrow stuck in the tree trunk. His facial expression spoke loudly. This had not been a dream.

Schultz shook himself off and spotted his horse grazing a few yards up the trail. He squinted and rubbed his eyes. Where had his saddle gone? He groped at his holster. No gun. Panicking, he reached for his knife. Gone.

He took a look to the south from whence he'd come. When he turned a few seconds later to retrieve his horse, it had disappeared. These strange events were having their desired effect.

Spirit Talker and I exchanged glances. It was time to conclude our hunt. My Comanche brother had outfitted himself in full regalia along with warpaint that only the devil could love. He appeared in the exact spot where Schultz's horse had been standing but moments before. "*Peeka tabu*," intoned Spirit Talker.

As Shultz was fully transfixed by Spirit Talker's appearance and fearful of what it might portend, he wet his pants as my arrow whizzed past his head and joined the other one in the tree. A deep growl from a hidden Zeb further distressed him. He looked about in a panic.

Finally, I was done torturing the man. He was about

as evil as they came, a murderer at the very least. The spirits of Gordon Small, Brawny Jones, and perhaps others yearned for justice. I emerged from the trees. "Are you ready to meet your Maker, Rolf Schultz?" I said.

"You?" he blurted.

"You are a murderer. I'm taking you to Sheriff Hoffman."

"You can't prove nuthin'," he insisted in a decidedly shaky voice.

"Don't have to prove anything. You're going to confess," I assured him.

"Not a chance," responded Schultz.

"You recall the last time we met on the trail, and I said I'd kill you? Well, it's your lucky day, Schultz. I don't want your blood on my hands. It's not the Christian thing to do. I'm taking you in to stand trial."

Spirit Talker had dismounted and now moved silently directly behind Schultz. He grabbed the man's hair and placed his knife against his forehead.

"Ever seen a man scalped while he still drew breath?"

"You wouldn't!" declared Schultz fearfully.

Spirit Talker made a surface cut along Schultz's hairline. It was just enough to send blood dripping down over his cheeks and lips.

Shultz flinched at the taste of his own blood.

"If you don't confess, my Comanche friends will seek you out." I gave him as threatening a look as I could. "Have you heard of Comanche tortures?" I said.

"Tie his hands," I said to Spirit Talker while keeping my arrow aimed directly at Schultz's belly. "Don't try anything. I assure you that this arrow is poisoned." Zeb came up alongside me and growled at Schultz. "Zeb doesn't like poisoned meat," I added.

Schultz was giving off an unattractive aroma owing to

having relieved himself in his own pants. I decided he'd have to endure it all the way to Bandera. "Let's get him on his horse and head to Bandera," I advised Spirit Talker.

"Why not kill here?" he asked.

"White man's law, my friend," I said with a sigh. I'd as soon be rid of the lawbreaker sooner than later, but vigilante justice was simply wrong. I had given a fleeting thought to setting Schultz on the trail naked and vulnerable. Perhaps a mountain lion or bear or wolf would do what we could not. But the outcome was too uncertain. If he were found and rescued, there'd be more troubles from him. No, he had to be duly tried, convicted, and likely hung according to the law.

We soon had him tied to his horse and began heading for Bandera. It had been a good hunt.

TWELVE
ANTIDOTE?

SCHULTZ WAS HARDLY the antidote to the poison spreading throughout the nation. Nor was he a model captive. Having been taken in by our deceptions on the Pinta Trail, he strove to make our lives miserable on our journey to Bandera. We put an end to his raucous, out-of-key singing by tying a bandanna over his mouth. His demands for frequent stops to answer nature's call were just about as annoying as his singing. Nevertheless, we stayed the course.

I still had no idea as to who was financing Shultz's venture. On occasions when we removed the bandanna, he revealed nothing. He did manage to spit a litany of threats to kill us and assurances that he'd never hang.

After two days of Schultz wearing at us with his ravings, we arrived at the outskirts of Bandera. I hadn't been here since winter. I naively reckoned we might see my friend August Klappenbach. But first things first. I urged Big Red forward. This time Spirit Talker accompanied me into Bandera.

Passersby offered varying reactions to us. Some gawked

at our caravan of me in the lead with Schultz's horse behind me, Zeb trotting alongside, and the wild Comanche pulling up our rear. A few folks recognized Schultz and voiced murmurs of support for us having brought in the man many rightly viewed as a troublemaker. Other folks, obviously fearful of the man, slinked away furtively. I heard a couple of whispers of "only good Injun is a dead Injun." Still others, believers in Schultz's pro-slavery rantings, gave Spirit Talker and me threateningly accusatory looks. We reined in before the sheriff's office.

"This is it, Schultz. You'd better not disappoint me." I pulled him roughly from his horse.

Spirit Talker slipped from his pony and followed Schultz and me into Sheriff Hoffman's office. I prodded the prisoner with the muzzle of my rifle.

Hoffman was nestled comfortably behind his desk, sipping some of the black slop he loosely called coffee. He barely flinched at me and Schultz but he spit coffee and nearly came out of his chair at Spirit Talker's entry. "What the!" he spewed. "No Injuns in…"

"Howdy, Sheriff. We brought you a gift." I waited while he settled back in his chair. "I've made a citizen's arrest of this man, Rolf Schultz, for the murders of Gordon Small and Brawny Jones. He has promised to confess his crimes before God and man."

Hoffman stood and laid a hard gaze on Schultz. "This true Rolf?" He glanced at Zeb, sitting patiently but intimidatingly at the door. There was nothing like the presence of a great gray timberwolf to ensure peaceful proceedings.

The sheriff's familiarity with using Schultz's first name was concerning to me. "Tell him, Schultz. Tell him what you admitted to me."

Schultz glanced around. He saw Spirit Talker's hand resting on his knife. The cut across the prisoner's forehead was still fresh both in reality and memory, as were the accompanying threats. "Yeah, Sheriff, I done in Small, the lying newspaperman. But I didn't kill the Jones fellow."

I nudged Schultz with the muzzle of my rifle.

"I hired a man to steal back my horse. He killed Jones."

"Makes him an accessory to killing, right, Sheriff?" I asked rhetorically.

Hoffman sighed, glared at Schultz, and grabbed a ring of keys from the wall. "Rolf Schultz, you are under arrest for murder and accessory to murder." He pointed toward the cells and marched Schultz to the first cell.

I missed Hoffman's wink at Schultz, but Spirit Talker saw it. My Comanche brother didn't miss much. But he said nothing.

Hoffman closed the cell door and returned to us. "The judge will be in town in about two weeks, Mr. O'Toole. You can bring any evidence and witnesses to trial at that time."

"Thanks, Sheriff," I said. Somehow, I didn't feel totally confident, given Hoffman's body language.

"Between you and me, O'Toole, I'd keep your Injun friend out of town. Only folks around here hate more than abolitionists is Injuns." It didn't register with Hoffman that Spirit Talker understood every word he'd said.

"Comanche no scalp," retorted Spirit Talker with his face contorted in a mock threat. He grinned and shook his head. "White man no change," he lamented.

Hoffman's jaw dropped. He stepped toward Spirit

Talker, but a quick growl from Zeb gave him pause. "Er…
y'all have a nice day, Mr. O'Toole."

"I'll try to protect the fine citizens of Bandera from
my friend, Sheriff," I said sarcastically upon exiting the
jailhouse.

As we prepared to lead our horses up the street to
Klappenbach's store, Spirit Talker paused. "Sheriff let
Schultz escape," he stated flatly. "Not keep in jail."

"How can you be sure?" I asked.

"He close one eye to Schultz. He not lock cell door."

Hoffman had winked at the prisoner! His placing him
in a cell to hold him for trial was a sham. "Doesn't leave
us much choice," I observed.

Spirit Talker made a cutting motion across his throat.

I nodded. "He must escape first. Then he'll be a
wanted man on the run." I nearly choked on my statement, as I realized Schultz hadn't been officially charged
or stood trial. So far as the sheriff was concerned, Schultz
was a free man unjustly brought to him and falsely
accused.

Spirit Talker shook his head.

Who was I to pass judgment and render punishment?
I'd be no better than the vigilantes that had tried to lynch
me. Here I was trying to build a better world with my
underground railroad and ridding the frontier of evildoers
while considering evil acts myself. I nodded at Spirit Talker.
"Maybe we can let God's justice prevail." I felt confident
that Schultz would eventually make the mistake that
would spell his end. Evil never went unpunished for long.

We hitched our mounts in front of Klappenbach's
store. As we were about to climb the stairs, we were
interrupted by a man leaning back in a chair on the
gallery. "You brought in that Schultz fella, did yuh?"

came the calm voice. The speaker was dressed in typical cowboy duds but with an especially broad-brimmed hat. He chewed on a piece of jerky.

We paused. I nodded. "Yep," I said and was about to continue into Klappenbach's store.

"He's gonna get out and kill yuh. Y'all kin be sure of that," said the cowboy.

There was something familiar about the cowboy's voice. "Do I know you?" I asked.

"Might not," retorted the cowboy. "I wrangle beeves fer yer neighbor Sam Collins." He smiled. "My name is Colt Crockett." He stood and extended a hand.

We shook hands. It was at this moment that I noted the big Colt Navy revolver hanging from his holster and a second stuffed into his waistband. I sensed that Crockett was more than a cowhand. "Is Sam in town?" I asked.

"Nope. He sent me to git a handle on feelin's around these parts."

"You mean the slavery business?"

Crockett nodded. "Nasty ain't it?"

"Well, we're making a quick visit with our old friend August Klappenbach and then heading out."

"You be the one runnin' that underground railroad, ain't yuh?"

I had taken a step toward the door. I paused and nodded. "That's what some folks say."

"Schultz is aimin' to kill yuh fer it."

"Guess I better watch my back," I replied.

"He'll bushwhack yuh fer sure, Mistuh O'Toole."

I offered a grim smile. "He's failed a couple of times. I'm ready for him." I nodded and proceeded into the store.

"Well, I'll be! Great to see you, Jack," called Klappenbach from behind a stack of women's clothing.

"Anything there that will fit a beautiful wife?" I chortled. "Those duds sure won't fit you, August."

"I see you brought your friends. Right bold," he said with nods to Spirit Talker and Zeb.

There was little like a fearsome Comanche in full regalia and an over-sized timberwolf to cement a secure mood for a meeting of old friends.

"You looking for a gift for Blue Flower?" asked Klappenbach.

I nodded, then turned to Spirit Talker. "You need anything for Topsannah?"

Spirit Talker began to walk among the rows of merchandise, while Klappenbach kept a friendly but wary eye on him.

"Word's already out that you brought Schultz in. Betting money says he'll never see a trial."

"That's what I suspect," I responded resignedly.

"You meet my friend out front?" asked Klappenbach.

"Sam Collins's hand? Yes, we met him."

"He's a hired gun," stated Klappenbach flatly.

"I gathered as such. Things sure are heating up about this slavery business." I rooted through some women's unmentionables and came up with something frilly. "I've already heard that Schultz will escape and try to hunt me down."

Klappenbach shook his head at what I'd chosen for Blue Flower. "Not her thing, Jack. May I suggest a fine pair of boots?" He pointed to shelves with rows of cowboy boots. "And you're right about Schultz."

Meanwhile, Spirit Talker had found a simple cotton dress for Prairie Flower.

"I'd advise you both to put some distance between

Bandera and home before Schultz escapes," counseled Klappenbach.

I placed a pair of boots on the counter along with the dress for Prairie Flower. Then I paused and stared at the cabinet behind Klappenbach. A brand-spanking-new Sharps Model 1859 lever-action falling-block percussion rifle sat there waiting for me. It was a single-shot, breech-loading piece using black powder cartridge ammunition. Importantly, it afforded awesome accuracy at very long ranges. "And I'll take that," I said, pointing to the Sharps.

"Merchandise is on the house, my friends, except for the rifle." Klappenbach took my money and handed me the Sharps. "I'll toss in the ammo, Jack. Now, y'all git and ride safe-like."

"Thanks kindly, August. Hope to see you again soon. Maybe, folks up high will find an antidote to the poison sweeping the land."

As we departed Klappenbach's store, Crockett hailed us. "If y'all be headin' north, mind if I ride with yuh?"

With the prospect of dealing with Schultz again, I reckoned it wouldn't hurt. "Sure. Get your cayuse. We're heading out now."

Crockett headed for the livery while we walked behind. As we passed the jail, there was not yet any evidence of an escape by Schultz. I did see Sheriff Hoffman watching us from the window.

THIRTEEN
ESCAPE FROM BANDERA

WE COULDN'T GET out of Bandera fast enough for my liking. I reckoned that Hoffman would keep Schultz jailed overnight at least. How soon the lawbreaker would come after me likely depended on how angry the evil creature was. As I thought on it, I'd fought off mountain lions, bears, rattlesnakes, hiders, slave catchers, Indians, bandits, vigilantes, and more. Somehow, Rolf Schultz had worked his way to the top of the list of my foes. He wasn't even especially cunning. He was a bought and paid for rabble-rouser devoid of morals. By my thinking, he was beyond redemption. I wondered whether God sometimes placed people like Schultz on earth to offer a contrast to the truly good people in His creation. I was pleased that Crockett had wished to join us, as it did add to our security.

I had managed to grab a newspaper from Klappen-bach's store as we departed and looked forward to perusing it once we found a place to camp. I was determined to catch up on what was going on beyond the confines of Central Texas.

We managed to ride far enough to have crossed the Medina River twice, as it meandered through the hills. Rising Cross Ranch would be reached in another day's ride.

Before the light faded, I broke out the newspaper and began reading. I ignored the disapproving looks from Crockett and Spirit Talker, as they set camp. We'd picked a reasonably secure spot beneath an overhanging rock. I had to kick out a couple of rattlers, or more accurately, eliminate them.

The news grabbed my attention. I tended to look first below what folks called *the fold*. Headlines were important, but the juicy news was often lower on the front page. One article claimed that nearly four million slaves existed in what they called slave states. South Carolina and Mississippi had the largest percentage by state. Texas ranked pretty much in the middle with an estimated one hundred eighty thousand slaves or nearly a third of our population.

I decided to sneak a peek above the fold. Abraham Lincoln was running for president against Democrats John C. Breckinridge and Stephen A. Douglas, and an outsider named John Bell ran as the Constitutional Unionist Party candidate. This being a Texas newspaper, it spoke none-too-kindly about Lincoln being an abolitionist. Breckinridge was the current Vice President and running to follow James Buchanan's presidency. There were no kind words about Lincoln. I sought relief by turning the page. An outfit called the Pony Express had begun carrying mail from Saint Joseph, Missouri to Sacramento, California and the Paiute tribe was at war in Utah Territory. I read that civil war had come to a close in Mexico with Benito Juárez dethroning Miguel Miramón. The newspaper editorialized that Napoleon III of France was formulating plans to invade Mexico and seat Austrian Archduke Maximillian in place of Juárez. I found the intrigue fascinating. Skipping to the third page, I was taken aback by a series of editorials supporting slave state secession from the Union.

"You gonna read that thing all night, Jack?" teased Crockett.

Spirit Talker simply waited patiently for me to finish and provide a summary of anything of importance.

I gnawed on a roasted piece of rabbit that Spirit Talker handed me and took a sip of coffee. "Nothing about Indians. Some fellow from Illinois named Abraham Lincoln is anti-slavery and running for president. No matter to me, since I can't vote. Says that electing Lincoln could touch off states leaving the Union. Oh, and that fellow Juárez in Mexico might soon be facing problems from France. Dang, but Mexico is a mess. Always rebellions!" I took another chew of rabbit.

"You been settin' there, an that's all there is?" observed Crockett.

I laughed. "About all that matters."

We finished dinner and doused our cooking fire. There was no sense in advertising where we were to the world, especially with the possibility of a vindictive Rolf Schultz picking up our trail. By my reckoning, he'd be too much of a coward to stalk us by himself. He'd likely hire a gun or two. So far, we'd managed to escape from Bandera unscathed.

I was on second watch a bit after midnight with Zeb sleeping beside me, when a stillness crept over the landscape. No coyotes howled. No owls hooted. Even the crickets seemed to have ceased their chirping. I didn't especially like what I wasn't hearing. It even awakened Zeb. It seemed far too soon for Schultz to have caught up with us. Who might be traveling at night? A bear? A lion?

I threw a stone at Spirit Talker. He awakened and looked up at me through sleep-deprived eyes.

I placed a finger over my lips and made a circle motion with my hand to indicate that something or someone was near.

Spirit Talker awakened Crockett.

Were we being stalked? Would we be passed by? Spirit Talker and I notched arrows in our bows. If danger lurked, we much preferred the bow and arrow. Even the click from pulling back a revolver hammer was too loud.

Zeb's ears were up. He was frozen in place and ready for action. Whatever was out there was taking its sweet time approaching.

"Got food?" came a gravelly voice from the darkness. It had a familiar timbre.

"Come in with hands high," I ordered.

An elfin figure with hands raised silently walked through a moonbeam in front of our campsite.

"Cutter Kincaid?" I called.

"None other."

"What you doing so far from your home?"

"Slavers tore it down. I barely escaped."

"Who's this?" asked Crockett.

"An old friend fighting against slavery," I responded.

"He be a little short," observed Crockett.

"I'll beat yer head in smart aleck," assured Kincaid.

"Nasty little beast," persisted Crockett.

Cutter Kincaid grabbed a large stick from the ground. "Say agin'?" he challenged.

"Easy, Colt. He's a friendly." I turned to Kincaid. "Might have a cold piece of roasted rabbit?"

Kincaid waddled on into our campsite. "Where y'all headed?" he queried.

"More like escaping Bandera," I replied. "But otherwise headed for home. Our companion here is Colt Crockett from the Circle C Ranch."

"Thet be Sam's place. He be a straight shooter," said Kincaid, plopping himself before the ashes of what was our campfire and beginning to gnaw on a rabbit leg. Noting that the fire was gone, he looked up at me. "Y'all runnin' from somethin'?"

I nodded. "Troublemaker named Rolf Schultz is fixing to kill me."

"Ah-ha. I be hearin' of him. Old Mississippi money."

I'd suspected Schultz was financed by some Southern aristocracy money. Given that Mississippi had a lot to lose if slavery were abolished, it was no surprise that they would stir up whatever hate and discontent they could against abolitionists.

While I was chewing on my thoughts, Kincaid stared over at Zeb. "Bet he'd love to take a bite out of Schultz," he said with mock seriousness.

"Schultz *isa wasu*," observed Spirit Talker.

"Poison indeed," responded Kincaid.

"You know Comanche language?" I asked.

"Helped keep my scalp these thirty years," said Kincaid with a laugh.

I scanned our gathering: a Comanche shaman, a gunfighter cowboy, a dwarfish frontier throwback, and me. Oh, and a wolf. We sure 'nuf made for an odd team.

Spirit Talker hushed us. "Listen!" he warned.

We heard the distant baying of dogs.

"Persistent devils," uttered Kincaid. "Sorry to bring this on y'all."

I looked at where Zeb had been sitting. He was gone.

Crockett was watching me. "What you thinkin', Jack?"

I smiled. "Cutter's dog problem might be over right soon."

Off in the distance, we heard the barking, then the yelping and squealing of dogs taking a whipping. It wasn't but thirty minutes or so, and Zeb reappeared. Blood dripped from his fangs, but he stood unscathed. I could barely hear the frustrations and lamentations of men whose dogs had been killed or totally cowed by the sudden attack by a wolf pack. Their hunt for Cutter Kincaid was ended.

"Owe yuh one, Jack," said Kincaid.

Crockett tipped back his hat and scratched his head. "Tain't seen nothin' like it!" he exclaimed. "Yuh do got that medicine, that *sunipu* stuff, Spirit Talker talked 'bout."

"Lord be praised," I responded. What more needed saying?

"Sun rise soon," observed Spirit Talker.

I gazed over to the east. "Let's relax for a couple of hours. It'll be good for us and for the horses."

———

ROLF SCHULTZ SWUNG OPEN the unlocked cell door. He'd done some serious thinking as to how he might rid himself of me and my Comanche friend. This had become personal. He nodded and winked at Sheriff Hoffman, as he sauntered out the jailhouse front door. The cut across his forehead was still too tender to put a hat on and the holster he'd strapped on was empty. He'd have to buy a new revolver and ammunition at Klappenbach's store. Schultz figured he needed a couple of men that were handy with guns and wouldn't run off at first signs of trouble like the two that had recently abandoned him on the trail. He reckoned to begin his recruiting at the saloon. A swig or two of whiskey wouldn't hurt either.

We had escaped from Bandera but not from Rolf Schultz.

FOURTEEN
WHAT NEXT?

WE BROKE CAMP. We had no mount for Kincaid. He insisted on walking rather than doubling with one of us. While it would slow us down, I reckoned it was preferable to have him with us if Schultz brought trouble our way.

When my concerns over Schultz weren't on my mind, my thoughts strayed to home and my loving wife, Blue Flower. I prayed all was well. We wend our way along a trail that could barely be called one. We mostly found ourselves picking our way single file through ravines, arroyos, grasses, cacti, and stands of live oak, occasional mountain laurel, and mesquite. We ducked low-hanging branches now and then. I admired Kincaid, as he trudged along among brush taller than he.

"How'd them Blacks work out fer yuh?" Kincaid's question brought me to the here and now.

"I haven't heard. Shorty taught them barely what they needed to know for the drive to Nebraska Territory." I laughed, as I recalled the surprise that had apparently escaped Kincaid. "Did you know that one of the Blacks was a woman?"

Kincaid froze, turned to me, and looked at me atop Big Red. "Yer kiddin'!" he declared with his hands on his hips. "How'd yuh handle that turn?"

I laughed. "Worked out. She wanted to be a cowboy, so we gave her the opportunity. She was a wisp of a little thing but did right well."

"I didn't know," offered Kincaid.

"She'd have likely blown away in a stiff breeze," I said. "Shorty can find other work for her if wrangling beeves on the trail gets too tough. Our cookie Perez could use help."

"Glad she gets a chance, Jack. Yer a good sort."

Spirit Talker had been riding a close-in point and pulled up. "No like path ahead," he whispered. "Go this way." He pointed eastward up a steep hillside.

I glanced down at Zeb. His ears were perked up. Something ahead had troubled him, too. I figured it couldn't possibly be Schultz. There was no way he could gain a day on us traveling through this terrain.

We reached the top of the hill and gazed out at what would have been the trail ahead. What appeared to be a Kiowa hunting party rode on through. If they saw our sign—and I'm sure they did—they must have figured we weren't worth pursuing. Our sighs of relief were short-lived. I took a look at our backtrail. Far off, I made out at least four riders. Were they Schultz and some new hires? At the pace they were traveling, their horses had to be tired. They were obviously aiming to catch up to something or someone. Me?

"Let's go," urged Crockett.

"No," I said. "Look yonder." I pointed to the distant riders. They were on a course that would intersect the

Kiowa hunting party. Soon enough, we heard gunfire. I figured that even if it was Schultz and they made it past the Kiowa, they wouldn't all make it.

Like many battles with Indians, it didn't last long. We soon saw the Kiowa galloping northward below our vantage point. At least two were wounded and barely hanging on to their ponies. One riderless pony was with them. There was no telling what had happened to the four riders they'd engaged. As if to answer my question, a trailing warrior charged by waving a fresh scalp.

Spirit Talker and I exchanged glances. We were thinking the same thing.

I led our little band down the hill, but turned southward at the bottom.

"Wait, where yuh goin'?" asked Crockett.

"We must see to those riders. Might be someone hurt."

"You forget about Schultz?"

"I don't think they could have been Schultz and his men. He hadn't enough time to put together a gang and catch up to us. It won't take us that long." I nudged Big Red down the trail, and everyone followed.

———

THE ATTACK LOCATION spread along about a hundred yards of trail. We first came upon the man who'd been scalped. I was surprised to see that he wore a uniform. He was near death, as he bled profusely from the head and four arrows protruded from him. Any single arrow would have been fatal. Two riderless horses stood ahead at the trailside. A man had staggered off a few feet and fallen. It was clear from his total and the arrows in his body that he was dead. Further ahead, two uniformed riders headed our way. They had apparently escaped the attack and were now heading back to check on their companions. They pulled up a few yards short of us. They didn't look pleased to see us.

"What are y'all doing here?" asked a soldier with three stripes on his tunic sleeve.

"Just travelers, Sergeant. We saw y'all had trouble so doubled back to see whether we might be able to help. My name's..."

"I know yer name," interrupted the sergeant.

"We spotted you from yonder hilltop. What y'all in such an all-fired hurry for?"

"That's Army business," responded the sergeant.

The truth came unexpectedly, as three camels emerged from the thick stand of live oak nearby.

The sergeant laid an angry glare on the beasts.

I recalled that the Army had been experimenting with camels at Camp Verde. Apparently, these beasts had escaped. I tried to suppress a laugh. The camels had cost the Army two lives. "My deepest sympathies, Sergeant."

"We'll take over from here, Mr. O'Toole."

I was about to turn northward but sensed the sergeant had more to say.

The sergeant gave me a concerned look. "Y'all might hurry. That Schultz fellow is making bad business about you in Bandera."

"Thanks for the advice." We reluctantly left the two soldiers to their sad duties. I felt reassured that I had sympathizers among the Army. I suppose word had gotten back about how well we treated a couple of their soldiers-turned-drovers.

We still had no horse for Kincaid but hurried along as quickly as we dared. He did quite well despite his short, bandy legs. He became the eyes and ears at the rear of our caravan, though we periodically paused to let him catch up. A downside for Kincaid was that when we stopped to rest, he'd catch up at just about the time we were ready to move on.

WE WERE about a mile out from Rising Cross under a panoply of stars, when Zeb took off at a run. About the same time, Big Red caught fire, as his ears went up and he nickered and snorted. I couldn't hold him back. Maybe, he sensed that his mares were near.

Kincaid was dead tired and dragging himself along. He waved us on. I needed no further prodding and let Big Red open his stride to a full gallop. Crockett and Spirit Talker fell in behind, though couldn't keep pace with my big stallion.

As I reined in before our house, Blue Flower already stood on the gallery with a welcoming smile. I leaped from the saddle and buried Blue Flower in my arms. "I missed you," was all I could muster.

"Boys sleep," she cautioned and planted a kiss that melted my parched lips.

Spirit Talker rode in a few seconds later with Crockett right behind. I shushed them, so the boys wouldn't awaken. "Crockett, the bunkhouse is over yonder." I pointed. Spirit Talker headed to the side of the barn where he'd spend the night. It was a few minutes before a huffing and puffing Kincaid arrived. We had all arrived safely.

"*Ana o'a hi'it*," whispered Blue Flower.

Kincaid perked up. Yes, we were hungry.

"We eat at bunkhouse," she directed, and she shooed off all but me. "Come help," she said with one of her fetching smiles that melted my knees. Her pregnancy was just beginning to show, but that mattered not a hoot to me.

Blue Flower pulled me inside and handed me a pot. "Water," she directed, then smiled. "Later," she cooed.

We soon had whipped up a stick-to-the-ribs beef stew. I actually felt sort of proud to have contributed. I lugged the pot to the bunkhouse. Crockett had lit lanterns, and Kincaid and Spirit Talker set a table.

"You joining us?" asked Crockett with a wink.

I shook my head. "See y'all in the morning. We'll have to decide how to handle Schultz. Get some rest while you can." I figured Crockett would head on to the Circle C. I'd loan Kincaid a horse, so he could continue to wherever he hoped to be free of the folks chasing him. Soon enough, it would be Spirit Talker and me taking on Rolf Schultz.

I wasn't going to let concern about Schultz ruin my homecoming, so headed back to the house and Blue Flower.

———

ANGRY FOLKS TEND to make mistakes, and I reckoned that Rolf Schultz was in a major lather as concerned me. I stood as testament to his failure. He'd likely figured by now that many folks were laughing at him behind his back. My parading him into Bandera as a prisoner had been the icing on that cake.

As I sat on the gallery taking in the morning sun and sipping coffee, I was painfully aware that I'd made a mistake in turning Schultz in to Sheriff Hoffman. It confirmed my assessment of Hoffman as a political animal that swayed with the wind that held power over him as he perceived it.

"Gonna head out, Jack," said Crockett, appearing as if from thin air with horse in tow.

I'd been so focused on my reflections on Schultz that I hadn't heard or seen him approach. I took a sip of coffee and nodded. "Give my regards to Sam," I said. "Pleased to have had you with us yesterday."

"You see it too, don't you?" offered Crockett.

"See what?" I responded, although I knew what he was referring to.

"If that Lincoln fella gits elected, there's gonna be hell to pay. I can't say as I cotton to slavery, but folks aroun' these parts are gonna have to decide which side they be on."

I admired Crockett's concise assessment of our situation. "You're right, Colt. I hope it doesn't happen too soon." I stood at the gallery rail and toasted him with my coffee cup. *Vaya con Dios, amigo.*"

Crockett mounted up and headed off toward the Circle C.

No sooner had Crockett ridden from sight than Cutter Kincaid waddled up to the gallery. He had a smallish mare in tow. "Whatcha want fer her?" he asked.

I slowly sipped the last dregs from my coffee cup. I enjoyed savoring the last drops, likely because they held the flavor of the coffee bean the longest. "She's my gift to you, Cutter. Tack, too," I responded.

"I be mighty grateful, Mr. O'Toole."

"I expect those folks that were chasing you are on the lookout for any sign of you. You might do well to seek out the McGregors up in Fredericksburg."

Kincaid laid a thoughtful expression on me, as he

considered my advice. "Yuh likely be right." With that, he managed to grab the saddle horn and swing himself up into the saddle. His athleticism was downright amazing.

"Sure you couldn't do with some coffee?" I invited.

"Yer Comanche friend brewed some concoction that set me straight. But thanks." He began to turn his mount but paused. "Good luck with that Schultz fella y'all were talkin' 'bout."

"Expect we'll need some luck. Got to count on the good Lord in that department." I responded.

As I watched Kincaid ride off, I half expected Spirit Talker to appear. He didn't disappoint.

"*Ana o'a hi'it,* my brother?"

He nodded vigorously.

"Blue Flower has breakfast about ready. Guess we need to talk about that Schultz fellow." I headed inside with Spirit Talker following.

The cabin was humming with activity. George and Isa were toddling around, and Peter lay wide awake in his cradleboard, surveying the goings on. The delicious aromas of breakfast were irresistible.

I had explained to Blue Flower all that we now faced with Schultz. I almost wished we had gone on the trail drive. If all had gone well, Shorty and the herd would be closing in on George's ranch up near Fort Laramie about now. But we were here at Rising Cross and must face whatever came our way.

Spirit Talker sat while I poured coffee. "You vote for Lincoln?" he asked.

I chuckled. "I'm not old enough to vote."

"Comanche vote in counsel when become warrior," reminded Spirit Talker. "Jack warrior."

I sure wished that was the measure. Despite my efforts

at building Rising Cross Ranch to a size that would enable me to wield influence in Austin, I still couldn't vote. There was no way around that. Blue Flower couldn't vote because she was a woman and a Comanche. Considering the troubles that appeared to be brewing, none of this likely mattered here in Texas. I sighed, as Blue Flower placed a heaping platter of ham, eggs, and biscuits before us. I was about to dig in when Spirit Talker touched my arm.

He bowed his head. "Thank you, God, for food. Amen."

Blue Flower smiled at her brother as she joined us at the table. "How Topsannah? How Buffalo Hump?"

"Topsannah with child," offered Spirit Talker with a smile. The smile faded. "Buffalo Hump old. Not well."

"Must visit soon," she said, then looked at me with a serious expression. "What we do about bad man?"

"This Rolf Schultz is angry. Angry men make mistakes. He likely has pulled a gang together. We have no idea how many men he will have. They will be hired guns that he's paying money for. Their loyalty will be only as good as what he's paying them plus any lies he's told them about me."

"What we do?"

I glanced over at Spirit Talker. He continued to eat but was listening intently. "With Hardy here to watch over our livestock, I think it'd be a good idea for Mukwooru and me to do some scouting. Once we know what we're up against, we can decide what to do next. If he's got too many men for us to handle, I'll send Isaac to get help from Sam Collins. I'm not sure whether we can expect help from the Texas Rangers. I understand that Rip Ford is returning from chasing Cortina, but we can't count on Ranger help."

Spirit Talker nodded. "Is two days to Bandera. Schultz no move too fast. We find."

Once we found Schultz, we'd be making a judgment call as to whether we'd take him on out on the trail or come back to Rising Cross for reinforcements. "We'll go right soon," I said decisively.

Blue Flower looked resignedly at me. Her man would have to defend the family again. This was the price she paid for my stand against slavery. It tested her mettle as a frontier-savvy Comanche woman. No matter what, she supported me.

———

I HAD DONNED buckskins for our scouting mission. They offered great camouflage in the wooded hills between Rising Cross Ranch and Bandera. I wore my 1851 Colt Navy revolver and a Bowie knife. Thanks to Klappenbach, I'd added an upgrade to my arsenal that I now unveiled. I caressed my newly acquired Sharps Model 1859 lever-action falling-block percussion rifle. It would be ideal if we ran into trouble, as it afforded incredible accuracy at long ranges. For our scouting, I left my bow and arrows at home. If we got close enough to Schultz to use them, it would be too close for comfort.

While I chose to ride Big Red, Spirit Talker traded his pinto pony for a dappled gray gelding that would blend in better with our anticipated surroundings.

Spirit Talker had managed to acquire a Remington Maynard conversion rifle. It was a slower load than my Sharps, but packed a wallop.

The crystal-clear summer day would afford us excellent visibility. Of course, that went for Schultz as well.

I kissed Blue Flower and my sons goodbye, and we

hit the trail. I'd shared our plans with Hardy and received assurances from Isaac that he'd go to Sam Collins's spread and recruit a couple of his hands in case Schultz packed greater numbers and firepower than we presently could muster. I kept reminding myself that this was now truly life or death. Anything Schultz brought had to be dealt with lethally. It was clear that he was beyond redemption.

FIFTEEN
A COMEUPPANCE

SPIRIT TALKER and I rode southward, retracing the trail from Bandera. We were all eyes and ears, as we wended our way with painstaking care through the trees and grasses covering the hills and valleys of the hill country. Zeb was on high alert and stayed close. I was of a mind that God had a special role ahead for my wolf companion.

We rode roughly fifty feet apart so as to afford us a better field of vision. I reckoned we were some fifteen miles from Rising Cross, when I brought Big Red to a halt and slipped from my saddle. I motioned to Spirit Talker to do the same. The distant sounds of jingling spurs and squeaking saddles came to us plain as day. If it was Schultz, there was nothing stealthy about him. If we could hear him, it could be that he could hear us. The fact that we were downwind was in our favor.

I saw a rock outcropping nearby, and we made for it as silently as possible. I'd only had one opportunity to practice with the Sharps but felt confident as I set myself to possibly use it. Being a heavy gun, I wasn't especially worried about recoil. The .50-caliber round exiting the muzzle would sure make a mess of whatever it hit.

I'd had the presence of mind to take the telescope with me. I'd roughed its cylinder such that it wouldn't grab the sun's rays and give us away. I took a gander in the direction of the sounds. They were maybe a quarter mile off. There were three men picking their way up the trail, but Rolf Schultz wasn't among them. It seemed as though they were simply cowpokes and likely headed to their next wrangling job.

I handed the telescope to Spirit Talker. He saw the same men I had seen but then raised his sight line farther down the trail. He handed the telescope back to me. "Three ride far behind," he said.

A couple hundred yards beyond the three travelers rode three more men. Schultz's black hat and the black stallion with white forelock were unmistakable. Now, the question was whether the three riders ahead of Schultz were part of his gang. They were all a good piece off but within range of the Sharps. Then again, I wasn't going to bushwhack anyone until I knew their intentions. The men with Schultz were obvious hired guns, but I couldn't be certain of the trio closer to us. "I'm thinking we should find a better place to defend. What do you think?" I asked Spirit Talker.

He nodded.

We mounted up and headed northward at a brisk pace to find high ground with a great field of view plus a path for escape. All the while, my mind was working on a strategy. So far as we could tell, Schultz had no idea that he and his gang had been spotted.

We found an ideal place to defend and hunkered down to wait for Schultz. "I'm not comfortable shooting first," I confided in Spirit Talker.

My Comanche brother was nothing if not succinct in his response. "No choice. No wait for *wutsutsuki* to strike."

He was right. You didn't wait for a rattlesnake to strike. I sighed. "We'll shoot men at Schultz's sides. I'll take the one on his left." Whether they were killed outright or wounded, it would send a crystal-clear message to Schultz.

We set the barrels of our rifles on tree branches to afford steady aim. The three riders came into view. Schultz and his two outriders had closed the gap with the trio riding in front of them. "Ready...one...two...three," I said through clenched teeth. Our rifles exploded as one.

My shot hit the rider to Schultz's left square in the neck, nearly decapitating him. Spirit Talker's shot went low and killed the horse of the rider on Schultz's right.

Mayhem followed. The three front riders turned and galloped toward Schultz. One swept up the unhorsed man as they swept past. Schultz turned with an angry expression and followed them to get out of range of our ambush.

I signed to Spirit Talker to head out. Despite our momentary weaponry advantage, we were still outnumbered five to two. I didn't feature getting into any extended battle. We mounted up and sought our next spot.

By now, Schultz was likely thinking back on how we'd harassed him on the Pinta Trail. He surely didn't want to be lured into a running battle where we'd pick off his men one at a time. However, he was also angry and thus not necessarily thinking straight. It would be his choice.

We set our next position about four miles up the

trail. We expected that our prey would be extra cautious now.

———

WE WAITED PATIENTLY. I periodically scanned the area south of us for any sight of the gang. We didn't have too long to wait. I sighted five riders moving cautiously toward us. They were spread out so far as the trail permitted, with anywhere from ten to twenty feet between the riders. The initial attack had confirmed that the three riders in front of Schultz were part of his gang. Still I was glad we hadn't fired at them until we were certain of their loyalties. Loyalties? They were only as good as the money Schultz paid.

We began to hear voices. "Yuh gotta up the pay, Schultz!" called out one of the outriders.

"Yeah to that!" called another voice. "They be havin' big guns wherever they be!"

"Five hundred!" called Schultz. "Another thousand to the man who kills O'Toole!"

"This be creepy. Ain't worth my life," said one rider. "I'm turnin' back, fools!" he added as he headed his mount southward.

Angered by the resistance, Schultz turned, aimed his revolver over the man's head, and fired a warning shot. "Ain't nobody leaving!" he hollered.

I nodded at Spirit Talker. The men were close enough. Dropping at least one more from his gang just might be enough to cause the others to abandon Schultz. I took careful aim. The explosion from the muzzle of my Sharps was heard shortly after the slug had done its damage.

Schultz's gang was being picked off one by one by an

enemy they couldn't see. His hired guns had enough and lit out at a gallop.

Schultz sat his saddle a tad too confidently. He wasn't so angry that he couldn't figure that we'd intentionally scared off his men. Two were dead, and the others didn't intend to wind up that way. But Schultz had not been our target just yet.

I observed him through the telescope. His eyes searched the surrounding landscape as though hoping to find us.

"Come out, you cowards!" he finally shouted. "You lily-livered bushwhackers!"

We remained silent.

"Face me man to man!" he called.

I glanced over at Spirit Talker.

He shook his head. He knew that it wouldn't be smart to face a man like Schultz mano-a-mano.

Schultz began to ride toward where he figured we were hidden. He was about fifty yards from us when he dismounted with rifle in hand. "I'm going to kill you, O'Toole. And your Indian friend, too." He was close enough that I could make out the veins popping out on his anger-reddened neck. "Death! I'll kill you both!" He screamed and began randomly shooting toward where he thought we were hidden. A couple of his bullets sizzled past our heads but all were well off target.

He was so wrought with rage and intent on killing us that he was oblivious to Zeb's charge. My great wolf companion threw his huge body into Schultz. There was no chance for him to defend himself, Zeb's jaws were at his neck. The end came quickly.

Spirit Talker and I ran from our positions toward Schultz. By the time we reached him, Zeb had just about finished him. Blood gushed from the evildoer's neck.

Schultz's eyes looked wild with panic for but another moment, then his body trembled, and his eyes closed in death. Zeb sniffed the body. He had no taste for human flesh, especially one so poisonous as Rolf Schultz. In a way, Zeb had proven an antidote of sorts.

"Let's strap him over his horse and take him back to Bandera," I said to Spirit Talker.

He gave me a questioning look.

"I don't want Sheriff Hoffman accusing me of killing Schultz. His torn neck will be proof that no human took his life."

It was an ugly task, but we wrapped Schultz's body in a blanket and tied it over his saddle.

"What about other men?" asked Spirit Talker.

"I don't expect any trouble from those cowards. There's no money in it for them. If need be, we can pay them with whatever money Schultz has."

"No Zeb in Bandera," advised Spirit Talker.

I nodded. Zeb had never been leashed, but if he followed me into town, there'd be trouble. Hoffman would demand that the mankiller wolf be put down.

With that, we headed for Bandera. Rolf Schultz had gotten his comeuppance, and I had managed to avoid having to end his reign of hatred and murder.

———

I WAS ABOUT AS RELIEVED as I was pleased to head home after delivering Schultz's remains to Sheriff Hoffman. Given the way Schultz's neck was shredded by wolf fangs, the sheriff didn't blink an eye at our story of finding him on the trail. We never did encounter the ne'er-do-wells that the man had hired. Hoffman had seemed as though a great load had been lifted from his shoulders to have the entire episode with the trouble-maker resolved. There were enough passions stirring about without someone like Schultz around inciting violence.

Zeb even endured being tied to a tree while I took care of business in Bandera. So far as I was concerned, he lived up to his name—a gift from God.

SIXTEEN
NO END TO POISON

"*TOSA* STILL HATE COMANCHE," blurted Spirit Talker, as we sat alongside our campfire roughly a day's ride from Rising Cross Ranch.

"*Tosa* hate pretty much any folks that aren't *tosa*," I responded. "*Tuhubitu, Ootupitu, Ohapitu, Ekapitu*—Black, Brown, Yellow, Red—doesn't seem to matter a hoot."

Spirit Talker looked off into the distance. "Jack no see color of skin."

I gave a knowing nod and said, "Not all *tosa*."

"God say we love. Men need God words."

I couldn't have agreed more. "We must teach our children love," I added. I laid back against my saddle. "Sometimes must teach tough love."

Spirit Talker looked over at me. "Jack know tough love."

He had me there. I'd sought to forgive some pretty evil folks during the times Spirit Talker and I had ridden together. Sometimes forgiveness and mercy worked and sometimes, as with Schultz, it didn't. "You heading home to Topsannah?"

"Two, maybe three days," he said wistfully. He looked up at the moon. "Mukwooru think Whites fight each other. Big fight."

He was predicting that all the passionate hatred swirling around for and against slavery would come to a breaking point with a great war. I couldn't imagine such a thing, or maybe didn't want to. "Not sure what we'd do, if that happened," I said. It hadn't occurred to me what we might be called to do if such a cataclysmic event happened.

"They call Jack to fight," said Spirit Talker thoughtfully.

He was right. I would have to take a side and likely be pressed to side with those defending slavery. Morally, I couldn't do that. I'd eventually have to face a choice. There seemed to be no end to the poison that was slavery.

———

IT WAS great to be home. With the Schultz episode behind us, I felt able to finally relax—at least so far as running a cattle ranch permitted anything resembling relaxation.

Talking with Spirit Talker about a possible war had been thought-provoking, to say the least.

I hadn't lost sight of my mission of battling slavery. Assuming that Shorty had reached George's ranch with most of the herd and lost no drivers, we'd would have managed to help six former slaves to freedom. It seemed a paltry number given the hundreds of thousands of slaves in America. Spirit Talker and I had no further discussion on the matter, though it weighed on our minds.

We sat at breakfast the day Spirit Talker was going to head home when an idea struck me. I looked at Blue Flower as she fed Peter. "Shorty should be back in about month, assuming no delays," I said. "Once he's back with Buck, Will, and Perez, I'm of a mind to head to Austin and meet this Sam Houston fellow. Hear tell he's fixing to be governor."

Spirit Talker simply stared at me for what seemed like an interminable length of time.

Blue Flower swallowed hard but seemed otherwise nonplussed. Her husband was thinking ambitiously again, though with great purpose.

In the silence, I could hear Zeb's breathing.

Finally, Spirit Talker's lips spread into a broad grin. "Jack strong *sunipu*."

"I reckon to learn the lay of the land. The political winds seem threatening. Maybe, they'll listen to reason." I found myself expressing my thinking out loud. "I hear Rip Ford is back in Austin. He knows me from Little Robe Creek. He could be a help." Little did I know that Ford's newspaper was publishing pro-slavery news.

―――――

THE MONTH ROLLED BY MORE QUICKLY than expected. That tended to happen when you had plenty to do. I was out on the north range one morning, keeping a wary eye for trouble. Hardy was about fifty yards off. Ever since the vigilante trouble, we'd maintained a hard and fast rule about riding the ranch in pairs. Fall was just setting in, bringing an early-morning chill with it. Early-morning chill translated to not quite hot enough to cause you to sweat.

I hummed a little tune by way of herding five longhorn strays. They were a persnickety lot of cattle, but my lullaby pretty much kept them calm and agreeable.

Hardy rode over with a smile on his face. "Heard a strange sound, boss."

"Where?" I asked.

"Over here. Musta been yer singin'," he said with a laugh.

I had quickly learned to have a sense of humor around my hands. I found it satisfying that they felt comfortable enough around me to even make me the butt of jokes. Part of my openness was my ever-increasing self-confidence. Everyone knew how tough I was and—more importantly—how I had everybody's backs. Loyalty coupled with faith in God ran strong among us. I began to laugh at Hardy's joke, when I saw figures riding off in the distance to the west of us. "You make them out, Hardy?" I asked.

He strained his eyes and then shook his head. "No, boss."

It occurred to me that I had my trusty telescope in my saddlebag. I pulled it out and took a gander up the trail. My jaw dropped. "It's Shorty!" I said almost loud enough to stampede the beeves.

We knew better than to make a sudden move to ride out and meet them. The cattle would have taken off. I looked through the telescope again. "Looks like all of them plus..." my words trailed off. Sheesha was riding with them. My mind raced with curiosity.

"I'll take these pretty beeves in, boss. Go ahead and ride on out."

"Thanks, Hardy," I said and eased Big Red to a walk until far enough from the five fidgety longhorns that we could pick up our pace. I even spotted Perez's wagon a ways off to the rear. It took about ten minutes for me to close the distance. Shorty waved his hat, and Buck sported a big smile. Will's expression revealed how relieved he was to be back and likely craving Kate's waiting arms and cooking. Sheesha rode just behind Shorty but made no eye contact. Perez was getting all he could from the tired oxen.

We all converged in a cloud of dust. "Welcome home!" I shouted. I gazed out upon a handful of very happy folks.

"Good to be home, boss," replied Shorty.

I turned Big Red and led the way toward the bunkhouse and barn. "Y'all made good time. I'm looking forward to hearing all about the drive."

"We're hungry, boss. Skipped breakfast. My belly and backbone are bumpin'." Shorty had a special way of saying he was starving. "Right tired of jerky an' that pemmican junk."

We rode fast enough that we nearly caught up with Hardy and the herd of longhorns that had just reached the pasture beside the barn. We were soon unloading the pack horses and wagon. A cowboy always cared for his horses before himself. I'd alerted Blue Flower and Kate of the arrival of hungry cowboys. Sarah joined in to help.

As we finished unpacking, I pulled Shorty aside. "What's with Sheesha?" I asked.

Shorty grinned. "She's gettin' hitched."

I gave him a questioning look. "To whom?"

"Not to me, boss." He laughed at the relief sweeping my face. "She's in love with a man still on the plantation."

"A slave?"

"Sorta," he replied.

"What's that mean?" I couldn't help but ask.

"He's a mix-breed. One of them indentured fellas."

"Mix? Indentured?" I pressed.

"She says he's a mix of Black, Cherokee, an' White. He be no slave. As I unnerstan' it, he can be bought out of his situation. Sheesha wants to marry him and take him back up toward George's place."

"We'll have to talk more," I said. "Sounds as though it's a question of money."

"Pretty much, boss."

———

SITTING around our hearth after dinner and hearing tales of the cattle drive was entertaining as much as informative. Though the weather had been tolerable, the drovers had dealt with one prairie fire and a handful of nasty thunderstorms. Blessedly, they'd faced no Indian attacks, though they had to trade away some beeves in exchange for safe passage. James and Frederick worked out well as drovers and eventually became friends with the other former slaves up near Fort Laramie. Even Sheesha held up right well driving doggies north. They told of a run-in with an angry grizzly and having to fend off coyotes and a pack of wolves. I laughed that the wolves must not have heard of Zeb's truce with humans.

I was especially interested in the Indian agent Thomas Twiss. I knew he'd taken a Lakota wife and had a couple of children by her. Shorty shared that Twiss wore his hair braided in two braids just like the Indians. Twiss owned livestock and chickens, hiring Indians to hunt for him in exchange for living accommodations and clothing. He'd brought in some White folks to tend his modest herds. Twiss had become like some sort of king, a tad big for his britches. Knowing that he'd made political enemies, I reckoned his lifestyle would spell his doom as an agent.

In turn, I shared how we'd eventually ended Rolf Schultz's reign of terror, made friends with a hand from the Circle C, and helped Cutter Kincaid. Sheesha stared fearfully at Zeb as I described his role in ending Schultz's evil ways.

Blue Flower tapped her coffee cup on the table to get our attention. "We help Sheesha?" she implored. Having heard the Black woman's story, she felt that we were obliged to help her.

I had already given the matter some thought. If we took Sheesha back to the plantation she'd escaped from, it would put her in great danger. It occurred to me that the only way we could free her man would be for me to purchase his indentureship. "What's his name?" I asked, turning to Sheesha.

"Samuel," Sheesha responded. She looked at me with grateful expectation upon realizing that I was fixing to help her.

"I think this is something I should do alone. I'm hoping to see my old friend Captain Ford and maybe get to meet this Sam Houston fellow." I had gotten to thinking that while I was still too young to vote in Texas, I had become a man of means. We were now ranching better than a hundred and sixty thousand acres a mere two days west of Austin. Wealth equated to influence so far as Texas politics was concerned. I'd be turning twenty years old in a couple of months, and I'd be voting soon enough.

Blue Flower smiled her approval. "Sheesha grateful," she whispered with a nod to the former slave.

Sheesha was quite dark-skinned as Black folks go, but I could see that a blush had swept her face and neck.

"I'll reckon to leave in a couple of days. I'll need the particulars about where I'll find Samuel and whomever holds his indentureship. I'd like to get that done before winter hits. I have a feeling this may be a cold one coming on." I took a final spoonful of venison stew and drained my coffee cup. I turned to my hands. "Y'all rest up from your travels, there's plenty for y'all to be doing around here. Shorty, we need to add to the corral, the one for horses. I want to raise some prime horseflesh. Also figure to look into some other cattle breeds. It'd be great to get a breed with more meat on their bones."

"Makes sense, boss," Shorty replied hesitantly.

"What's on your mind?"

"Longhorns still be a hearty breed out here. They be rangy, but they resist them ticks and handle the range right well."

I nodded. "I won't do anything without checking with you, Shorty." I knew that it was important that I respect the expertise of my foreman.

"About time to turn in," observed Perez. The exuberance that accompanied the arrival home had worn off. The men were dead tired.

The men filed out, each thanking Blue Flower and Kate and complimenting their cooking skills.

Buck was the last to head for the door. He paused before heading to the bunkhouse. "Let's talk tomorrow, big brother." He gave me a wink and exited.

I could only wonder what might be on his mind. He was nearly fourteen, but growing up fast. You had to, out here on the Comancheria. Shucks, he'd just returned from a trail drive. That'll grow a young man up right quickly.

Ordinarily, my thoughts would turn to trying to get a meeting with this Sam Houston fellow. It just might take a bit of finagling. Houston was one of those folks who become a legend in their own time. With his victory over Santa Ana at San Jacinto a couple of dozen years back, he'd secured Texas independence and become the Republic's first president. He dealt with all the problems concerning a fledgling nation and became its first governor upon joining the United States in 1845. He went on to represent the state in the US Senate and, having returned to Texas. He was odds on to be elected governor to replace Hardin Runnels. I'd heard that Houston had some slaves but wasn't sure where he stood as to abolition. Blue Flower's tug on my arm broke me free of my erstwhile strategizing.

"Jack, come," she said, dragging me away from the kitchen.

SEVENTEEN
CHANCE MEETING

I HAD DECIDED to travel light. That meant no packhorse and everything I might need strapped to and behind my saddle. The weather had become a tad nippy lately, especially in the early morning hours. I was sticking to my prediction of a colder-than-normal winter, whatever normal was.

Big Red nickered and snorted with the excitement of once again heading out on the trail. We were soon headed east toward Sam Collins's Circle C spread. I worried about Sheesha. I feared a slave catcher might find her.

We reined in at the Circle C around mid-afternoon. The cabin spoke of hard times, but I admired Collins for enduring. The front door swung open just as I slipped from my saddle. "Sam! Good to see you!"

"Why, Jack O'Toole! Same to you, pardner," he responded. "Coffee's on." He motioned me to come in.

I helped myself to the coffee and joined him at a small oak table. A fire smoldering in the hearth kept the place comfortably warm and shed a glow around the room.

The place sure could have used a woman's touch. He'd lost his wife, so I figured to not broach that subject unless he brought it up.

"What brings you here?" asked Collins.

"Heading for Austin. Reckoned I'd pay you a visit, my friend."

"Anything in particular happening?" he pressed.

"Hope to catch up with Captain Ford and maybe wrangle a meeting with our soon-to-be-governor Sam Houston."

Collins nodded and took a long sip of coffee. He stared thoughtfully at me. "Still fighting slavery?"

"Matter of fact," I responded with a serious gaze over at the fire. "I fear for the nation, what with folks starting to talk of leaving the Union."

"Wish you luck, Jack. The folks with the power have slaves, lots of slaves. They need them and fear them. Sam Houston's not likely to resist the slave owners."

"It doesn't seem right that we ranchers must yield to the plantation owners. We have no need for slaves even if we were inclined to own any. There are no shackles on cowboys working the range."

"What else you aiming to do in Austin?" Collins had a way of sensing that I had another purpose.

"You have me figured, Sam." I chuckled and took a sip of coffee. "I aim to look up a fellow named Burt Colthwaite."

"Colthwaite?" exclaimed Collins. "Nasty customer from what I've heard. You hear of folks who treat slaves well and those that don't. He's got a reputation for being mighty quick to apply the lash."

"I'll be looking to purchase an indentured man from him."

"That's a tall order, Jack," advised Collins. "He only respects strength, so don't be playing nice."

I swallowed the last of the coffee. "Thanks, Sam. I'd better be heading on."

"You can bunk here and start fresh in the morning," he offered.

"Appreciate the hospitality, but I'd best cover what ground I can before dark. Hope you can visit Rising Cross come Christmas."

"Thanks, Jack. Good luck with Colthwaite."

I was soon back on Big Red and heading toward Austin. I was glad that Zeb was with me, if for no other reason than he afforded friendly company that never talked back.

———

I WAS surprised at how Austin had grown into a bustling city. As I understood it, the population had blossomed to nearly thirty-five hundred folks. Of course, that didn't count Mexicans, slaves, or Indians, as they were considered non-citizens.

I hadn't a clue as to where to find Rip Ford these days. I reckoned I'd most likely learn his whereabouts at a local drinking hole. I headed for what might be best described as the seamy side of Austin where drunks and soiled doves might be found. I reined in before a saloon that I reckoned would afford me access to folks with answers as to where I might find Captain Ford. I took up residence at the end of the bar. While I chose not to imbibe, I ordered a whiskey and pretended to drink it. I knew that Ford had been appointed to head the Texas Rangers.

A soldier reeking of alcohol moved close to me,

smiled, and belched. "Pardon," he blurted and belched again. "You new to Austin?"

I shook my head. "Nope." Realizing that the man wore sergeant's stripes, I figured he might know something despite his inebriated condition. "Actually, I'm looking to find that Texas Ranger fellow, Rip Ford."

The sergeant looked down at Zeb through rheumy eyes. "That be a big dog, yuh got there, cowboy." He looked up as though suddenly remembering what he meant to say. "You don't know 'bout Ford?" he said with another belch.

I shook my head. "Know what?"

"Ford ain't in Austin." The sergeant eyed my whiskey. "Old Rip's been sent back to Brownsville to help the US Army win the Cortina War."

This was disappointing news. I thanked the sergeant and pushed my glass of whiskey toward him.

He looked pleadingly at me.

I nodded, and he gulped down the whiskey about as fast as I'd ever seen.

I wasn't too disappointed, as my hope of meeting with Ford had been chancy at best. By the time I finished my business around Austin and returned to Rising Cross Ranch, it'd be reported that shortly after Christmas, the Texas Rangers and Army defeated Juan Cortina's forces in the battle of Rio Grande City. It would effectively end all but minor harassments by Cortina's Mexican rebels for the next few years. Ford ultimately succeeded in ending the threat of any large-scale military incursions.

With my hopes of reconnecting with Ford dashed, I figured to seek Sam Houston. It wouldn't be worth my time to talk with Hardin Runnels, as his term as governor was coming to an end. I learned that Houston lived in Huntsville but did get to Austin. I reckoned to begin with the Texas governor's mansion, though Houston hadn't taken residence yet. Huntsville, where he and his wife Margaret Lea maintained a lovely home called The Woodland, was a five-day ride from Austin. I wasn't up to handling an extra ten days of travel along with the possibly time-consuming negotiations with Burt Colthwaite.

I ordered another whiskey and nudged it to the sergeant. The bartender described the mansion as having been built by Abner Cook a few years back and that it had eleven rooms and a couple of fancy outdoor privies. I hoped and prayed that Houston would be in town and that someone could direct me to him. I headed out with the sergeant, still looking in amazement at the size of my dog. I hoped Zeb wasn't insulted.

———

AS I APPROACHED the governor's mansion, I realized that Big Red was growing tired. We'd been pushing hard. I gazed longingly at the mansion and reluctantly turned toward a stable a short distance away.

"Any decent food to be found nearby?" I asked the stable boy.

"Ma Prickett's place is over yonder," he responded through a half-mouthful of teeth. "It's 'bout good as any, mistah."

"Thanks kindly. I'll be back in the morning."

"They might not take kindly to yer dog," he advised.

"We'll see, I said and ambled over to Ma Prickett's dining emporium. Well, it was more like a ramshackle hole-in-the-wall than fancy emporium."

Ma Prickett's was nearly empty. There was one other gentleman in the establishment, and he nodded as Zeb and I passed by. I had my choice of tables and found one off to one side with a seat facing both the entrance and the kitchen. As I waited for a server, I took a gander at the other patron. He wore a black suit with silk-embroidered vest, white shirt, and string tie. His broad-brimmed black hat sat beside him on the table with the crown downward. He sported highly polished boots with fancy spurs, and I couldn't help but notice the Colt revolver hanging from the holster on his hip. A cigar held loosely in his hand sent spirals of smoke upward. He appeared to be fully engrossed in a newspaper. I gathered he'd recently finished a meal, as he sipped coffee between draws on the cigar. He must have sensed that I was staring, as he looked up and gave me what seemed to be a friendly nod.

A young woman, Dolly by name, came and took my order of potatoes, eggs, and corn topped with biscuits and gravy. I added coffee as an afterthought and a piece of raw steak for Zeb. Dolly didn't seem bothered by my furry companion.

I sat looking around Ma Prickett's eatery while awaiting my order. I was bored.

The dark-clothed gentleman finished reading, stood, and looked my way. He was about my height. His dark features framed a dark mustache. He smiled. "You passing through?"

I nodded.

"Don't often see a tame wolf," he observed. He took a couple of steps my way. "I'm done with this newspaper," he said as he handed it to me.

"Thanks kindly," I responded.

"Sorry, but you look familiar. Ever ride with Rip Ford?"

I looked up. "Scouted for him at Little Robe Creek."

"I saw the way you walked more like woodsman than cowboy," he said friendly-like. "My name is Bat Mills. I fought the Comanche there myself."

"I'm Jack O'Toole. Wasn't much of a fight," I observed.

"Those Quahadi Comanche put up a good tussle. Plumb tuckered us out." He looked off as though trying to imagine the battle. "Rest of the savages got clean away. But we got a bunch."

Dolly arrived with my dinner.

Mills handed me a printed card with his name and address. "If you are ever in need of any legal assistance recovering property, feel free to contact me. I'm always up for helping a fellow Ranger."

"Thanks kindly," I said, then watched him leave. He seemed like a nice enough fellow, but I found myself wondering why a man in his line of work needed fancy spurs on his boots and carried a gun. Maybe he was a cowpoke on the side, I thought with a chuckle. Not likely, duded out as he was. I cut a piece of steak. It was so tender that my knife sliced through the beef like it was warm butter. It turned out that the stable boy had good taste in dining. I hoped the young man had good advice for lodging.

I wound up sacking out on a pile of hay in a corner of the stable.

TURNED out that Sam Houston wasn't in town. I learned that he was staying in Huntsville until his term as governor began. Two-thirds of my mission had failed thus far. I prayed I'd have better luck dealing with Colthwaite.

The morning temperature was brisk enough, though a fog draped itself over the landscape as I headed Big Red northward. I had a rough idea where to find Colthwaite's property, though couldn't see much more than a couple of hundred yards ahead of me.

I likely hadn't ridden more than a couple of miles out of Austin, when I made out a dark silhouette riding ahead of me. Big Red's long legs were gradually closing the gap between us, so I held us back just a tad.

We rode for perhaps an hour like that until he made a sharp turn eastward. I had a sense that it might have been the fellow I'd met at Ma Prickett's the night before. I shrugged and rode on.

The fog began to lift. That feeling I get when danger lurks led me to believe that I was being followed. I decided to double back to check my backtrail. I found a place with plenty of mesquite and tall grasses so as to leave the trail without whomever was following me seeing my tactic. Spirit Talker would have admired my skill.

The maneuver took about a half hour. Strangely, my tail turned out to be Bat Mills. He'd apparently doubled back to ride behind me. Thus far, it didn't appear as though he knew I'd back-trailed him. Was his riding the same trail as me a coincidence? I looked down at Zeb. His ears were on high alert. I reckoned to hang back and see where Mills was heading.

We rode on for about another hour before Mills stopped. He scanned the landscape around him, acting as though he'd lost something. Apparently, he'd lost me.

I was still following the directions given me to Colthwaite's place, but decided to follow a wide berth around Mills's position. I chose to travel downwind to minimize any chance of revealing myself, so I headed due east.

Soon, I figured that I was far enough away to head back for the trail.

The fog lifted by mid-morning. As I approached the trail to Colthwaite's plantation, I heard a rustling among the brush ahead of me.

A somber-looking Bat Mills rode out from the grasses and blocked the trail.

I didn't have a good feeling about this.

"Where you headed, Mr. O'Toole?" asked Mills.

I reined in Big Red. What business was it of Mills to ask where I was going?

"Young fella like you should be careful what he gets involved with," he said with a decidedly threatening tone.

I remained silent.

"Mr. Colthwaite would be none too pleased to see you. Your reputation precedes you, Mr. O'Toole."

How on earth did he know where I was headed?

Mills laid an evil glare on me. It was as though spikes of darkness were spewing from his eyes. "Turn around and go home," he growled.

I'd pretty much had enough. To my thinking, I'd dealt with his kind before and didn't appreciate being threatened. Mills didn't scare me. "You seem to know my business," I responded.

"Don't mess with me, O'Toole. It's my business to know. Go home." His hand began to hover threateningly over the butt of the gun at his hip. "Go, and no more trail tricks like doubling back."

I didn't move a muscle. It would obviously have been foolish to engage in a gunfight here on the open trail. For all I knew, he was an expert with that piece of steel at his side. We were too far away for Zeb to go into action. I heard a fluttering as some birds flew off.

"Look, I'm giving you a chance because you rode with Rip Ford. Don't push your luck." Mills was standing firm.

I had just about decided to take Mills's advice, when the click of a rifle hammer being pulled back broke the silence.

Mills heard it, too. He froze. His dark eyes tried to focus in on the source of the sound. His hand wrapped around the butt of his revolver.

An explosion shattered the air. Mills's body flew from his saddle. His horse lit out.

Big Red pranced about nervously but settled quickly. All became quiet again save for a few frightened birds still chirping their annoyance. But Mills lay face down on the trail, blood seeping from under him.

I looked around then heard hoofbeats trailing away. Who had shot Mills? I slipped from Big Red's saddle and cautiously approached Mills's body. With my Colt drawn, I used my foot to turn the body onto its back. The pallor of death hung heavily over Mills. I took another look around me. Whomever had killed Mills was long gone. Likely, the killer had saved my life.

I fetched a shovel from my pack. Even folks like Mills deserved a burial. Before planting him, I rooted through his pockets. There were more cards like the one he'd given me at Ma Pickett's, and he carried a couple hundred dollars in gold and silver. I found nothing on him as to next of kin. I feared encountering another sheriff like Hoffman back in Bandera who might accuse me of waylaying Mills. Right or wrong, I put the coin in my saddlebags. Perhaps, a church could make use of it. That having been said, I did say a few words over Mills's shallow grave.

With Mills off my trail, I proceeded onward toward Colthwaite's place.

AS I RODE ALONG, I was left to wonder who had shot Mills. Somebody out there wanted me to complete my business with Colthwaite on behalf of Sheesha.

The sun was nearing the horizon, as I rode within sight of the vast acreage farmed by Burt Colthwaite. There was no point in conducting business in the dimness of twilight, so I chose to make camp.

Having cold-camped so as to not alert anyone to my presence, I lay back under a starry sky and thought back on my adventures. I'd come a long way since the massacre of my ma and pa and my older brother and sister by Comanche. I was only fifteen at the time. My greatest challenge had been resolving the conflict between my feelings of guilt, anger, and revenge with my Christian values of love and forgiveness. I'd saved my younger brother and sister from Comanche kidnapping, made a lifelong friend of a Comanche, and even married a beautiful Comanche princess. The frontier had, by necessity, caused me to mature faster than most men. I was a rancher and a husband and father. I'd driven cattle northward, fought Indians, fended off lawbreakers, and survived attacks by predatory wildlife. My heart was gripped by concern over humans in bondage, causing me to take on a mission of combating slavery. In a mere five years, it seemed that I'd lived a lifetime. I felt a wet tongue slobbering my cheek. Morning had arrived, and Zeb was ready to greet the day.

EIGHTEEN
NEGOTIATIONS

TROTTING up the tree-lined path from the gated entrance to *COLTHWAITE*, I had to admire the surrounding beauty. A couple of bent-over Black men along the way glanced up furtively at me as they tended beds of flowers. It seemed rather grandiose for the man to emblazon his name across the arched header at the gate.

A two-story white mansion with four columns lining its front appeared in the distance. More Black folk scurried about. None seemed happy, though all were busy.

Far off to my left, I saw a man putting a whip to a chained Black man cowering under the blows of the lash.

Burt Colthwaite turned out to be the burly bearded man that greeted me on the steps of a house that made my cabin at Rising Cross look like a mere hut. There was no smile on the man's face. In fact, he may never have smiled in his entire life. He wore a white suit that threatened to burst at its seams. Guess he ate well. A broad-brimmed white straw hat graced his head.

I reined in a few feet from the broad stairway.

"Howdy. I'm Jack O'Toole and I'm looking for Burt Colthwaite."

"You're looking at him, boy. How'd you get here?" His greeting was not exactly a welcoming one. It was as though he knew I was coming but was surprised to see me. I began to suspect a connection between Colthwaite and Bat Mills. His eyes widened as he realized the animal sitting at Big Red's hooves wasn't a dog.

"Mind if we have a chat, Mr. Colthwaite. I've come to do a bit of business with you."

He coughed and blew his nose into a laced handkerchief. He raised an eyebrow. "Okay. I'll listen." He hailed a green-jacketed Black man nearby. "Claude, bring some tea." Colthwaite motioned me to join him on what he called the veranda. It was just a fancy name for a gallery or porch, so far as I was concerned.

"I own a ranch west of Austin, Mr. Colthwaite. We breed cattle and horses on about a hundred and sixty thousand acres." This was my way of letting him know that I wasn't some small-timer. "We've been finding it difficult to find cowhands. I was talking with a fellow in Austin, and he suggested that you might have some indentured folks that might learn to wrangle livestock."

Claude placed glasses of tea with mint sprigs before us.

Colthwaite took a sip of tea. "Who told you about me?"

"Saloon barkeep named Whitey at the place near Ma Prickett's."

Colthwaite chewed on that a moment. "You run into a fellow named Bat Mills?"

I shook my head.

The plantation owner seemed concerned, then he put his hand over his mouth. He rubbed his beard as if to camouflage a belch then wiped away spittle with his sleeve. "You say you're interested in indentured folk? No interest in some well-muscled darkies?"

"No place for slaves on a ranch, Mr. Colthwaite." I had begun to find the very presence of this man disgusting.

"I assume you are…" he said hesitantly.

"I have money, Mr. Colthwaite."

About this time, a comely young woman appeared at the door to the veranda. She was hiding a black eye behind a fan. Colthwaite heard her. "Come, Violet, and greet our visitor. Mr. O'Toole here is looking to purchase one of our indentured men."

Violet walked tentatively but gracefully to the man's side. "Miss Violet here, is my woman." He gave her a lascivious look that seemed to undress her where she stood.

"Pleased to meet you, Miss Violet," I said politely.

"Go ahead back in the house, Violet," ordered Colthwaite. "I'll see you after business."

I sipped the tea to gather my thoughts. I'd never experienced any situation like this.

"Claude, fetch Pierre, Michael, and Samuel." Colthwaite rubbed his pudgy hands. "We'll talk business out back, Mr. O'Toole." He seemed to have forgotten Mills or chosen not to pursue the matter.

We finished our tea and strolled to a fenced area behind the big house. There was a lashing pole with manacles and chains at the center of the enclosure. Claude escorted three well-muscled men to the enclosure.

Colthwaite waved off an overseer who was dragging a half-clothed woman behind him. "You can whip her later,

John. I've got business here." The overseer nodded and reluctantly dragged his captive away.

"This all you have?" I asked.

"These are prime specimens, especially Samuel here. He's a Black, White, and Indian mix I got from a trader in New Orleans. Paid five hundred for him. He's worked off maybe a year of his time. The other two come cheaper."

I made a show of inspecting each man. "They speak English?"

Colthwaite nodded. "Pretty much. The dark one over there named Pierre speaks French right well."

I noticed the Black girl being slapped down by the overseer as he awaited the availability of the lashing pole but mostly focused on the three indentured men. "I like this one." I pointed to Samuel.

"Seven hundred," blurted Colthwaite.

That translated to a small herd of longhorns. I smiled. It was never proper to accept an initial offer. I had drawn Bat Mills's money from my saddlebag. This seemed like an appropriate use. "Four hundred fifty," I offered.

"You can be on your way, O'Toole. That's downright insulting."

I turned to leave.

"Six hundred," he stated flatly.

I squinted at him. "Bit high. Let's close at five hundred and fifty." I extended my hand.

Colthwaite nodded and shook my hand.

I had an urge to wash my hand.

"You want him manacled?"

"Sure. And his papers and—of course—the key."

Colthwaite wiped his mouth with his sleeve again. "You're welcome to join us for dinner, Jack. You might consider spending the night and getting a fresh start come morning." He smiled deviously. "Violet has a right pretty sister whose company you might enjoy." He pointed up at a window from which a raven-haired woman with sad eyes watched us. "She'd make you happy," he added with a wink.

I felt as though he was wiping his slimy mouth on my sleeve. "Thanks just the same, but I'll be on my way. It'll take a few days to get home." I had an urge to throw up.

"Pleasure to do business with you."

I was about to turn away, but realized I needed a mount for Samuel. "Oh, how about a horse for Samuel here."

Colthwaite thought on that. "Got an old gelding you can have for only twenty dollars." He offered to shake hands again, but I tipped my hat instead. I forked over another gold piece.

I felt as though I couldn't get away from COLTH-WAITE fast enough. The entire experience had been sickening. As I walked away with Samuel chained behind me and Colthwaite walking alongside, I heard the first screams of the woman at the lashing post.

———

I RECKONED that we were a good seven miles or so from Colthwaite's clutches, when I felt clear enough to unfasten Samuel's manacles.

Samuel had been silent. Now, he looked at me curiously.

"You remember Sheesha?"

Samuel's jaw dropped. "Yes." It was the first word he'd spoken since I'd inspected him back at the plantation.

"She asked me to free you."

Samuel's eyes moistened. "She and I..." His voice trailed off.

"My name is Jack O'Toole. I help bring slaves to freedom. I was helping Sheesha escape but she returned to my ranch and pleaded for me to free you."

"Thank you," Samuel said humbly.

NINETEEN
ESCAPE

IT COULD BE SAID that Samuel and I were escaping. We couldn't get away from Colthwaite and the dark evils that permeated that plantation fast enough. I expected that his rough treatment of slaves and of those in his household were too common among his ilk. I'd heard of folks that treated slaves as family, but Colthwaite's methods couldn't be confused with that sort of thinking. Even Violet and her sister seemed to be in bondage to Colthwaite. I wished I could have freed all of them.

We camped near a creek and feasted on what remained of my jerky and pemmican. I did build a small fire and brewed some coffee.

"How did you become indentured, Samuel?" I asked as we stared into the flames.

"My father was Black. My mother part Cherokee and part White. Life in Carolina not good for mixed blood." He looked off to the full moon hanging high above us. "We hungry. When I was fifteen, my father was accused of stealing bread. He tried to escape, but was shot and killed. My mother and I ran. She got sick and die."

I guessed Samuel to be better than twenty years old. "What happened to you?"

"I did what you call drifting. Went to small farms and found work. I cleaned barns, picked crops, shoed horses, fed pigs. No money, but not hungry. After maybe three years, I hear of Texas. I could sell myself—what they call indenture—and buy my freedom. I dream of a farm or ranch."

"And Sheesha?" I asked.

"She favorite of master, but have eyes for Samuel. Master not happy."

I could only imagine how a vile excuse for a human like Colthwaite handled the situation.

"Me cost him much. No beat. Give me work slopping pigs." He stared with sad eyes into the flickering flames. "Master whip Sheesha."

"Do you love Sheesha?"

Samuel looked off dreamily at the stars then back at me. "Yes." He nodded.

"You believe in God?"

Samuel nodded. "Pray but He not speak to me until you come." He riveted his eyes on me. "Why you help Sheesha?"

"Slavery is wrong. No man should be in bondage to another. God intends us to be free." I picked up a stick and played its tip in the flames. "My mission is to free slaves."

Samuel looked at Zeb lying beside me. "Where you find wolf?"

"Zeb here? He found me," I said with a smile and ruffled Zeb's furry mane. "He is my gift from God."

Zeb licked my hand and settled his snout on my thigh.

"Zeb has saved me a time or two," I understated.

"You have what you call a ranch?" Samuel asked.

"Rising Cross Ranch is about four days from here. It's fair-sized. Many cattle and horses. My wife is of Comanche blood, and we have three young boys. My friend Spirit Talker is her brother." I reckoned that was enough about me for now, though Samuel seemed as though he wanted to hear more. "Let's turn in. We need a good night's sleep. I'll keep first watch."

"I can watch, too," said Samuel.

I hoped so, as I kicked dirt on the fire and settled in with my rifle across my lap and blanket around my shoulders.

———

"ANA O'A HI'IT TOSA!"

The Comanche words greeted my ears, as I tried to shake loose the cobwebs of sleep. I glanced over to where Samuel was to be keeping watch. He was asleep. A Comanche hunting party astride their ponies was staring down at me. I had to think fast. "Pohya Isa," I said, pointing to myself. "Penateka," I added.

The leader of the band gave me a curious look. "Muk-wooru *pabi*," he said with a look of recognition.

I breathed a sigh of relief upon them recognizing me as a friend to Spirit Talker. Apparently, they'd heard of Walks With Wolves.

"Noconi," said the leader. "Mamanu." He pointed to himself.

The leader's name translated to Mighty Warrior. The Noconi Comanche had taken the brunt of Rip Ford's onslaught at the Battle of Little Robe Creek. Spirit Talker and I had done our best to minimize the attacks on the Comanche tribes but were unable to help the Noconi.

"*Tosa kaahaniitu.*" I observed that the Texas Rangers had deceived the Comanche. I left out the fact that Captain Rip Ford's Tonkawa allies had guided the Rangers to the Comanche encampments.

Mighty Warrior spit. He didn't need reminding of the devious Tonkawa. The traitors had mutilated the dead Noconi Comanche after the battle. They respected neither man nor woman nor child. Mighty Warrior turned his attention to Samuel, whose reddish skin combined with negroid facial features was unusual to them. "*Numunuu ekapitu?*" He asked if Samuel was of the Indian people.

I looked over at Samuel. Despite his large, well-muscled physique, he was trembling at the sight and demeanor of the Comanche. I had to admit that they were a fearsome band, especially to anyone unfamiliar with their culture. "Cherokee," I said with a hand motion to Samuel.

"Cherokee," repeated Mighty Warrior. "*Tu taiboo?*" He wondered whether Samuel was a Black man.

"No *tu taiboo*. Come from many moons to rising sun." I signed, pointing eastward. With that, I offered what remained of our supply of venison jerky. It was meager at best.

That elicited a smile from Mighty Warrior. He nodded to his hunters, and a decidedly fierce-looking warrior rode from the rear of the band. Across his pony was a small doe. The leader motioned to give us the deer. "Pohya Isa no *hoikwa*. Brother to Mukwooru." He'd pointed out the obvious—that we hadn't hunted.

I accepted the offering. It was a fresh kill and had already been field-dressed. I signed my gratitude to Mighty Warrior.

"*Kuuna,*" said Mighty Warrior. "*Ana o'a hi'it.*"

I realized that we were going to make a fire, roast the venison, and share it among all of us. I must say that I should have expected this. I turned to Samuel. "Relax. They are friendly and wish to share the deer."

———

WE MANAGED to get through the meal with the Noconi. We laughed and shared stories of hunts and battles as best we could, given my limited knowledge of the Comanche language as supplemented with plentiful use of signing. Samuel was at a loss. He didn't even speak the Cherokee tongue. Thus it was that we got a late start continuing our journey to Rising Cross Ranch. On a positive note, we ate well and kept our scalps.

"You have Comanche friends?" asked Samuel, as we headed along what little there was of a trail.

"A few," I assured him. "The Indians are an interesting people. They are an ancient culture. They worship the spirits of just about everything. I have tried to teach them of God...of truth...of love. It's not easy."

"What of your friend...this Spirit Talker? And your wife?" inquired Samuel.

"Spirit Talker, called Mukwooru by his people, is a shaman or medicine man. I saved him from a mountain lion attack a few years ago, and we have been like brothers ever since. He believes in God and tries to get his people—or numunuu—to understand. As to Blue Flower, she was slow to accept Christ."

"You have children?"

I laughed. "Three boys. Isa and George are twins. They've just learned to walk and talk while Peter is still a baby. We expect another child in a few months."

"Jack lucky," observed Samuel. "Maybe Samuel have big family one day."

We rode on in silence. There was much to be said, but riding the wide expanse of prairie tended to encourage silence. I admit to having talked to myself and sung a few off-key ballads, but silence was the way most time passed on these days-long journeys across the frontier. I did manage to bag a couple of rabbits along the way home, so we didn't lack for fresh meat.

I expected to encounter travelers with the increase in settlement around Austin, but there were none save for a few distant wagons and a Kiowa hunting party. I reckoned it was attributable to the onslaught of colder weather.

I had started cogitating on how to handle holding an escaped slave at Rising Cross. It was a matter of what solution would be safest for us all. The fact that neighbors already suspected my abolitionist beliefs would serve to bring us extra scrutiny. I reckoned it would be best to get Samuel and Sheesha north as quickly as possible.

TWENTY
REUNION

RISING Cross Ranch came into view late afternoon. I'd chosen to not stop at Sam Collins's Circle C, as I was anxious to reunite the lovers.

Samuel's eyes were alight at the prospect of seeing Sheesha, but we headed for the barn. It was our first duty to care for our horses. I unsaddled Big Red, gave him a quick curry and some feed, and led him to his stall. As the gelding Samuel rode was released into the adjoining corral and we were exiting the barn, Sheesha appeared. I saw Shorty, Buck, Hardy, and Will clustered near the bunkhouse and smiling broadly. There'd been a bit of anticipation going on.

Samuel stepped forward hesitantly, but there was no holding back Sheesha. She flew to Samuel's arms to the accompaniment of clapping cowboys.

I reckon this made my trip to Austin a success, even though I never got to meet Rip Ford or Sam Houston. I glanced over at our house where Blue Flower was watching from the gallery. I carved a path wide of Samuel and Sheesha and strode over to Blue Flower's waiting arms. "I missed you," I murmured in her ear.

She took a warm-hearted look over her shoulder at the reunited couple as we eased inside. There, we could embrace without an audience—save for three boys demanding our attention. "*Ana o'a hi'it?*" she asked wistfully.

"Yes, I'm hungry," I sighed.

Meanwhile, Samuel and Sheesha had been escorted into the bunkhouse, where the cowboys had partitioned a section for the couple. It would have to do. Hopefully, they wouldn't have to endure the accommodations for long. While it might have lacked for total privacy, it would serve as adequate shelter from what could be harsh Texas weather.

I prayed that we'd get through the winter with Sheesha here at Rising Cross. It would have been fool-hardy to escort her to Nebraska with its prospect of blizzards and frigid temperatures.

———

OUR THOUGHTS BEGAN to turn toward Christmas. Despite our growing family and more ranch hands, we planned to uphold tradition and enjoy Christmas dinner around the great oak table in our house. I decided that we'd need some fresh meat. While serving beef was a natural, I reckoned to hunt down some deer so folks would have a dining choice. "I'm going to hunt," I mentioned to Blue Flower as I sat sipping hot coffee.

She nodded. "Maybe buffalo and antelope," she added with a laugh. Her humor could be very much like her brother, Spirit Talker.

"I'm taking Buck with me."

"He like that," she acknowledged. "One day, you hunt with Isa, George, and Peter."

That would be far off, but I loved her thinking. It was the Comanche custom that boys were under the tutelage of their mothers until they reached about twelve years old. From then, the men taught them the skills required to be hunters and warriors. "Seems we'll have many feasting at our table," I observed.

"We have plenty. Kate, Sarah, and Juan help cook."

I laughed, and Blue Flower looked at me curiously. It seemed that every Christmas we had one or more unexpected guests. "I wonder who our surprise guest will be?"

"No worries," she responded. "God knows."

———

ABOUT TWO INCHES of snow coated the landscape as Buck and I set out to bag some venison. If we could bring three home, it would be ideal. I had a hankering for venison sausage, and anything left over could be made into jerky.

One of the benefits of winter hunting was that some apex predators like bears hibernated along with poisonous reptiles. There were still javelina, cats, wolves, and coyotes to contend with, but Zeb gave us an edge over those critters. I liked to think that most stayed away as sort of a professional courtesy to Zeb. Zeb loved the hunt, because I'd reward him with a share of the kill. Wolves weren't carrion eaters, so fresh-killed meat was required.

I gave passing thought to hunting with bow and arrow, but my trusty carbine enabled prey to be brought down from a greater distance. Maybe, I was feeling old at age twenty, but I didn't much cotton to traipsing around the woods in cold weather.

"Let's ride to the hills yonder. What do you say, Buck?" I asked through a cloud of frosty breath while pointing at the rolling landscape that comprised some of the far southern reaches of Rising Cross Ranch. Not waiting for an answer, I nudged Big Red along while Buck followed on a roan stallion with a gray gelding in tow.

Buck had spent some of his pay from the trail drive on a new Sharps carbine and was anxious to unlimber it. "I'm with you, big brother," he answered.

We meandered southward through arroyos and ravines. The wind picked up a tad, and dark clouds began gathering to the northwest. I looked over my shoulder at Buck. He'd wrapped a blanket over his shoulders and was hunkered down in the saddle. I figured we were maybe five or six miles from the ranch house.

Despite the predations of settlers, game remained bountiful on the Texas frontier. It wasn't long before I spotted a small herd of a half dozen white tails about a hundred yards off. We were downwind, so that gave us some advantage. Gusty bursts of wind kicked up clouds of snow between us and the deer. I reined in and waited for Buck to come alongside. "They'll scatter on the first shot. If we fire at the same time, we'll bag two and get home ahead of that storm that's brewing yonder."

"W-w-works for me," said Buck through chattering teeth and casting suspicious eyes at the darkening clouds.

"You did practice with the carbine?" I questioned.

"Y-y-yes...a little," Buck responded. He didn't exactly inspire confidence.

I dismounted and drew my Sharps carbine from the

saddle scabbard. I patiently waited while Buck slid from his own saddle and grabbed his carbine. I led us over to a nearby live oak with a low branch that would be ideal for resting the barrel of a rifle to steady our aim. "I'll take the buck on the left, you take the doe on the far right," I whispered.

The deer were obligingly offering us broadside targets.

Buck struggled with his cold fingers to load a cartridge into the Sharps but was finally loaded and ready.

"Fire on three, Buck."

He nodded.

"One...two...three." Two explosions shattered the chill hill country air.

The buck fell where he stood. The poor doe struggled with a busted hindquarter. Desperate to ease her suffering, I slid a cartridge into my carbine and put her out of her misery.

"Sorry, Jack," lamented Buck.

"Let's dress them and get out of here," I said, ignoring his apology. I silently promised myself that I'd be sure Buck had plenty of practice before hunting again. I hated to see animals suffer needlessly.

We clambered over rocks and around scrub brush to the carcasses. Zeb beat us to it and was chowing down on the doe's rump by the time we got there. Ignoring my hungry friend, we went to work field dressing the deer, wrapping them, and tying them over the back of our packhorse.

An especially strong gust of wind signaled the proximity of the coming storm. "No time to waste, Buck. Looks like a blizzard heading our way." I didn't feature being caught up in any blizzard even close to home.

Blinding wind-driven snow could make finding our way even over familiar trails challenging at best.

We were about a mile from home when the snow began to hit. I was grateful to be able to keep Zeb's tail in sight ahead of us as snow, driven horizontally by the force of the wind, hit us from our left. Ice pelted our faces.

Well, we made it to the barn just as the full force of the storm hit. As I opened the barn door, it was nearly blown from its hinges. We got the horses inside and breathed a sigh of relief. We still had to deal with Buck reaching the bunkhouse and me getting to the ranch house. I hung the deer carcasses high from a rafter to keep them out of reach of any scavengers that might manage to find shelter in the barn. Horses cared for, Buck and I headed back out into the storm to traverse the short distances to our lodging. With the buildings south of the barn, the wind pushed us along right quickly. Squinting through the driving snow, I saw Buck make it to the bunkhouse and was relieved when Zeb and I reached the ranch house door. I managed to pry it open against the wind and squeezed through, followed by Zeb and a freezing cold blast of wind-driven snow.

Blue Flower was standing at the stove and looked nonchalantly over her shoulder. "Must you let cold air in?"

I stood there, mouth agape with melting snow beginning to drip from me. I couldn't miss her humor, but was ready. "Coffee ready?"

We both laughed. I threw off my buffalo coat, and we embraced.

"God watch over Jack and Buck," she said gratefully.

I nodded. "It's His timing," I agreed. "Buck and I bagged two deer to add to Christmas dinner."

"Bagged?" she asked.

"Killed. They're hanging in the barn."

Blue Flower poured two cups of coffee, and we went over to the window to peer out at the storm. The blizzard was beginning to look as though it was playing out. She snuggled close under my arm. "Two days to Christmas. Wonder who come?" she mused, looking up at me with a smile. "Blue Flower make bear sign. It still warm."

I smiled broadly. With warm, fresh sweets, she could get me to do just about anything.

"Boys sleep," she cooed with a wink.

———

NEXT MORNING, I wandered over to the bunkhouse through the ice-encrusted yard. Everything in sight was covered in crystals that the sun's rays made appear as millions of diamonds. I eased my way inside. Shorty, Buck, and the others were finishing breakfast and readying to head out to check for any damage caused by the storm. The stove in the center of the building made it toasty warm. The blizzard had been brief but harsh. The primary duty for the morning was to check our livestock. We'd built some shelters around the ranch but could only hope that cattle and horses had the sense to make use of them. They were stocked with hay to attract them, but sometimes that wasn't enough.

Sheesha and Samuel had made the best of the situation in the bunkhouse. Upon my entry, Samuel peeked from behind the privacy curtain. "Samuel marry Sheesha," he announced.

Everybody smiled knowingly, as though he'd better make an honest woman of her.

Samuel scanned the men. He shook his head and

wagged a finger, as if signaling that he and Sheesha had not consummated their relationship.

"How about if we have a ceremony after Christmas dinner?" I announced.

There were plenty of nods.

Sheesha emerged dressed to join the rest of the cowboys in checking cattle.

Everyone looked at her and smiled.

I cleared my throat. "I think Sheesha should stay home today and get ready for her wedding."

Samuel looked at her with a loving gaze. "Mr. O'Toole is right."

With a frustrated look at the gathering of men, Sheesha acquiesced.

"Come with me. I think Blue Flower can help you get ready." I waited while she donned a coat and then led her off through the snow to the ranch house while a smiling Samuel watched us depart.

I was right pleased that we'd have a special event at our Christmas gathering.

TWENTY-ONE
SLAVE CATCHERS

TEXAS WEATHER! It was hard to figure. December 25th, and the temperatures were decidedly mild.

We hosted a houseful of folks for our Christmas feast. Yep. Better than a dozen squeezed around our otherwise amply table to celebrate Christ's birth. Sam Collins even brought a couple of his hands, Colt Crockett and Hank Johnson. The ladies had laid out a spread fit for kings. The veritable cornucopia of culinary delights included roast beef, venison, potatoes, corn, biscuits, jellies, and more—much more. Pies—apple, blueberry, and peach— topped off the dining delights. Belches and groans signaled a surfeit of dining gluttony.

I stood and hammered the end of the table with the butt of my Colt to get everyone's attention. "We have a special event," I announced. I endured the personal embarrassment of a silent burp. Folks near me laughed but quickly grew serious under my arched eyebrows. "We are gathered here today to celebrate Christ's birth and to celebrate the beginning of new lives together." No one had noticed Sheesha and Samuel leave the dining table. I raised my hands as a signal, and they emerged from our bedroom dressed in wedding attire. I use the term *wedding attire* loosely, as Blue Flower and I had done our best to outfit the couple in frontier finery. Sheesha's black tresses had been carefully woven into a single long braid down her back, and she wore a white, colorfully beaded buckskin dress with matching moccasins. Samuel wore a white shirt with string tie, an ill-fitting black jacket I'd borrowed from Isaac, brown trousers, and black boots. His hair was slicked back. He appeared as nervous a groom as might be expected, while Sheesha was serenely beautiful.

While I wasn't a pastor or justice of the peace, and there were none for fifty or more miles around, the conduct of the wedding fell to me. I had thought back to the simple ceremony years ago at Buffalo Hump's encampment which mostly involved me handing over a dowery of ponies and followed by Spirit Talker blessing Blue Flower and me in God's name. I vaguely recalled something about someone giving away the bride, but that didn't seem to hold water here.

I motioned Samuel and Sheesha to stand alongside me. A hush fell over the gathering as I cleared my throat. "It is God's will that man and woman should live in marital harmony to love and support each other through good times and difficult times. Samuel, do you take Sheesha to be your wife?"

Samuel nodded nervously. "Yes."

I turned to Sheesha. "Sheesha, do you take Samuel to be your husband?"

She delivered a yes almost before I could complete the question.

"In Christ's name, I pronounce you man and wife. Samuel, you may kiss the bride."

Samuel was about to look about anxiously when Sheesha wrapped her arms around him and planted a kiss full on his lips.

The gathered guests went wild with laughter. Joy abounded.

So it was that we celebrated until there was a loud banging on the front door. A gunshot broke the festivity. "Git yer Injuns an' Nigra-lovin' people out here, O'Toole. An' yer half-breed swine!"

———

A SILENCE FELL among our guests.

Shorty and I cautiously strode to the front window. "I count eight," I said with a look over at my foreman.

"Heavily armed, boss. Bandannas over their faces and look to be drunk," observed Shorty. It appeared that some folks had been over-celebrating Christmas and not observing the Savior's birth.

I motioned for everyone to get down on the floor. If there was any shooting, I figured to minimize any injury. "Who goes?" I hollered from the window.

A gun fired, and a bullet plowed into the front door. Up to now, the only shooting had been into the air. Our visitors had turned ugly. "You come outta there, O'Toole! No gun an' hands high!"

I looked around the room. Our Christmas revelry had come to a decided halt. "Shorty, hand out whatever guns you can find, but don't do any shooting. I'm stepping outside." Blue Flower gave me a pleading look, but I had to face the pack of troublemakers. I stepped to the door.

"Don't shoot. I'm coming out." I cautiously opened the door.

One of the horsemen fired, and the bullet passed my head and into the doorjamb. I flinched.

"Whoever you are, get your men under control," I said firmly. "What do you want?"

One of the men, the apparent ringleader, rode forward about a horse's length. His bandanna had dropped just below his crooked nose such that I could make out a mustache. He wore a broad-brimmed black hat that cast a shadow over his eyes. "Hold yer fire!" he snarled at his companions. He turned his attention to me. "I said to git y'all out here," he demanded. "An I want that slave woman. She be worth a pretty price." He was a drunken slave catcher who didn't realize he'd come after the wrong folks.

I laid an icy glare on the man. "You come any closer, and there's going to be yours and a lot of your men's blood spilled." I let him think about the rifle muzzles poking from the window ports of the house. "Now, nobody is leaving this house."

The leader began to swing the muzzle of his rifle toward me.

"I wouldn't be doin' that iffen I were yuh," came a firm voice from the corral. There was the telltale click of a hammer being pulled back. "Any idea what size hole a musket ball can put in yer brisket? Yuh be dead right quick-like."

The leader froze.

I could see from his eyes that he was weighing his options. He and his men sat their horses out in the open yard. If shooting started, they would get the worst of it. It was a sobering situation. What he'd likely thought were easy pickings wasn't to be. The muzzle of his rifle slowly tilted skyward. "We be leavin'," he growled.

"Don't think so," I stated emphatically. "Drop your guns and slide from those horses."

A couple of the men hesitated, but one by one, they began to dismount. They laid their guns on the ground.

Shorty, Hardy, and Will moved from the house with guns on the interlopers. I looked over at the corral to see none other than Cutter Kincaid grinning from ear to ear. "Lower those bandannas," I ordered.

"I saw the tall one with the big mouth in Bandera a couple of weeks back, boss," called Shorty, pointing to the ringleader.

The gang leader looked at me as though fearing the worst.

"This being Christmas, it's your lucky day. I'm in a giving mood. You might say, I'm even in a forgiving mood. Your slave-catching days around here are over." By now, I hoped that the gang had begun seeing the errors of their ways, though anything was possible in their inebriated condition.

"Wh-wh-what yuh got in mind fer us?" stammered the leader.

I could smell the alcohol on his breath. "I'm figuring y'all have drunk too much and lost your senses. But…" I paused for effect. "But, y'all have threatened me and my family and friends. That isn't right, is it?"

All the gang nodded. Their eyes betrayed fear of what I was of a mind to do.

"By rights, we could string y'all up to yonder tree."

I could see a cloud of uncertainty and abject dread flow through the gang of troublemakers. The bullet that flew past my ear was heavy on my mind. But for that, their shenanigans had been mostly harmless, booze-fueled carryings on. Casting racial aspersions also stuck in my craw. As I thought on it, I couldn't very well let them go unpunished. Nothing I might say would be likely to change their prejudiced mindsets. "Shorty, tie them up."

Buck, Hardy, and Will pitched in to tie the men's hands behind their backs.

"I don't care whether your skin be White, Black, Red, or Brown, we're all human beings. Our nation's founding document says we have a right to life, liberty, and the pursuit of happiness. Y'all would do well to follow that sentiment." I looked at Blue Flower who gave me an approving nod. "Y'all understand me?"

"Yes sir," they replied nearly in unison.

"Shorty, turn them all backward on their horses and tie them in their saddles."

The deed was soon completed. I stood in front of them, surveying our handiwork. "Don't you men ever dream of ever coming back here." I turned to Shorty. "Now, guide them to the trail to Bandera and let them find their way." I waved them off.

They were a sad sight to behold—nine riders headed off single file. Their heads hung low at the error of their ways. I hadn't recognized them, though Shorty thought he'd seen the leader before in Bandera. It struck me how easy it was for men to be led astray. Had we not been sober and heavily armed, the outcome could have been tragic. The threats to us and others who opposed slavery seemed to be building. We were committed to keeping and obeying God's word, but I sensed that we'd be increasingly challenged by those who did not. We'd taken the narrow road of faith, while many others traveled a far wider road that encompassed a far-reaching range of sinful pursuits. I hoped the gang of rabble-rousers would never return, though I knew that slave catchers—whether sober or drunk—would still be plying the region.

Cutter Kincaid finally came strolling over.

"You're a sight for sore eyes, Cutter. Glad you happened by," I said.

"I was just tryin' to git here afore dinner," he said with a mischievous grin.

"Well, come on in, and we'll scrape some grub together for you."

"I be smellin' pie," he said with a laugh and led the way back into our house.

We all found our way back to the table. The incident had sure taken the edge from our Christmas celebration. Sheesha and Samuel breathed sighs of relief. She had wisely remained inside during the confrontation, as revealing herself might have incited a violent outcome.

We moved to the fireplace hearth, taking seats as space permitted. This was a ritual that our friend George Freeman had shared with us. Each person shared something they'd been grateful for from the past year. There was a lot of gratitude shared. Shorty, Perez, and our other cowhands, including Sam Collins and his cowboys, gradually headed to the bunkhouse to continue their Christmas revels with games and tall tales.

Soon, only me, Blue Flower, Kate and Will, and the newlyweds remained. I laid a couple of logs on the fire and stoked it a bit.

"I wonder how our troublesome visitors are enduring?" I ventured.

"Jack heart too big," suggested Blue Flower with a faint smile. She both admired and feared my tendency to forgive transgressors.

I stroked my chin thoughtfully as I stared into the

flames. Finally, I turned to Blue Flower. "I think big trouble for our nation is brewing. We must be ready to leave here, to leave quickly."

Blue Flower was taken aback. She intuitively knew this was eventually coming, but I had surprised her with the finality of my words. "Where we go? My *numunuu*?"

"No. Too close. We must travel north to George's ranch."

"Long trail," she observed. "What of Rising Cross?"

"Will and Kate can run it...if it survives." It was the first time I'd revealed serious doubt as to the future of our ranching endeavors. It sent shivers of fear through our gathering.

"You must stay strong, brother," offered Kate. "We admire your strong faith, what Spirit Talker calls *sunipu*, strong medicine."

We sat around and chatted about the good and bad we might yet face. Blue Flower was still a few months from birthing our fourth child. The hour grew late, and yawns took over.

"Let's call it a night. Merry Christmas, everybody." I took Blue Flower by the hand and led her away. Our sons were already sleeping. We had moved them from their bedroom and offered it to Sheesha and Samuel for their first night as a married couple. After that, it'd be back to the bunkhouse for them.

―――――

WINTER GAVE way to the spring of 1860 with not even a hint of further trouble from slave catchers, vigilantes, or other malcontents. Nearly all of our livestock survived the winter and were growing fatter on the lush spring growth of grass. Calving would begin soon.

Sam Houston was now governor of Texas. I was still of a mind to meet him, but life at Rising Cross Ranch was too busy for me to go gallivanting off. I had begun to think on finding more slaves to take to freedom, but until we were ready for another trail drive, that wasn't feasible.

The day finally arrived for Samuel and Sheesha to depart. They were intent on heading north to the North Platte country and a truly free life away from the threat of slave catchers.

They had worked at chores around the ranch over the winter, so I was pleased to gift them horses and a pack mule. Samuel wanted to reimburse me for paying off his indentureship, but I'd have none of it. We fortified them with plenty of supplies. Sheesha, having traveled the trail northward and back, would be the pathfinder for their journey. Theirs was a bold move by any measure.

"We are ever grateful for all you've done for us," said Samuel. He and Sheesha were a tad teary-eyed with gratitude.

"We're pleased that we were able to offer y'all a path to freedom. We hope and pray that your journey will be a safe one." Inside, my stomach turned over with deep concern for their safety. The frontier was a dangerous undertaking for experienced travelers. Even folks in large wagon trains risked life and limb to take on the arduous landscapes of the plains and mountains. Rivers had taken many souls, not to mention calamities like fires, storms, and floods. Wildlife like rattlers, bears, and wolves were a constant concern. As if all that weren't enough, there were hostile Indians to contend with. Sheesha and Samuel would have the added challenge of staying out of reach of slave catchers. They were a beautiful, happily married couple looking forward to a joy-filled life of freedom.

Shorty, Buck, and Hardy joined Blue Flower and me, escorting them to the northern reaches of Rising Cross Ranch. Once there, they headed on, plodding slowly into the distance, looking back and waving to us now and again. I prayed we would eventually see them happily ensconced near George's ranch up on the North Platte.

———

WITH SPRING CAME the need for replenishing essential supplies that we couldn't make or grow on the ranch. Blue Flower was but two months from delivering our fourth child, so we decided she'd best not make the three-day trip along decidedly rough trails to Fredericks-burg. It'd be Shorty, Hardy, Buck, and me. We would take turns driving the wagon and brought along a couple of extra horses.

The wagon was in great shape for our journey, as we'd learned a few things on the long trail drives with Perez's rig through mostly unforgiving territory. A spare wheel and spare axle were essentials, and we had extra water and plenty of axle grease. We rigged a canvas cover similar to that used on prairie schooners. Blue Flower even made a cushion for the seat. The wagon was the lap of luxury.

We weren't expecting trouble, as the Comanche and Kiowa had been fairly peaceful of late and I had the respect of most Indians in our part of the Comancheria. There was always the worry over bandits anxious to rob careless travelers. We took no chances, as we were all heavily armed. There was enough ammunition on us and in the wagon to likely defeat a small army.

I bade goodbye to Blue Flower and the boys, and we set out on a crystal-clear morning in early April. I took first turn driving the wagon, though Big Red wasn't over-joyed at being tied to the rear. Zeb sat beside me in the driver's box.

I'd gotten hold of a newspaper before we left Rising Cross so was up on some of the latest goings on. The nation's politics weren't pretty. The fellow from Illinois that the plantation owners feared would apparently be running as the Republican candidate. Abraham Lincoln would be opposed by any of several Democrats, the most talked of being John Breckinridge and Stephen Douglas. Yep, it sure was looking ugly. While slavery was at issue, it was camouflaged under political blather over states' rights. Would men's passions whipped to a fever pitch see through the ruse? Not likely.

We managed to reach the Pinta Trail and decided to camp. The temperature was pleasant and air dry. We built a good hot cooking fire and enjoyed venison from a young doe that Buck had shot during the day's travel.

"Do you think Sheesha and Samuel will make it to Nebraska?" asked Shorty.

They'd departed only a week before we left for Fred-ericksburg. By now, they should have journeyed well north of us.

"If they make it past Palo Duro Canyon, they should be in good shape," I responded.

"That's a big if," noted Hardy. "No telling what they might run into."

"Guess all we can do is keep them in our prayers," I offered.

WE WERE UP and rolling at sunrise, but not until we'd finished off the last of the venison and quaffed plenty of coffee. The Pinta Trail was not intended for wagons, so we'd have some rough challenges ahead. There was no time to waste. There was the Pedernales River yet ahead, and we didn't want to deal with a waterway fed by heavy spring rains.

It was past midday, and we'd managed to traverse about half the distance to the river. I was riding Point on Big Red with Zeb trotting alongside. I was about fifty yards in front of the wagon scouting for obstacles to be avoided and staying alert for human and animal predators.

I rounded a sharp bend in the trail that hid me from the wagon and the others. Big Red's ears pricked up, and Zeb went on full alert. Something was ahead of us that alarmed them. I looked higher and spotted a couple of vultures circling just above the treetops.

I decided to not wait for Buck and Hardy or for Shorty who was driving the wagon. I drew the Sharps from its scabbard, placed it across my saddle horn, and urged Big Red cautiously forward.

I was all eyes and ears as we moved forward. We came upon another turn in the trail. The sheer horror that came into view caused me to pull up short. What remained of two humans hung from a live oak branch. They had apparently hung there for a couple of days, as any stench had dissipated. Coyotes and vultures had begun their work.

As I sat surveying the scene, the boys pulled up behind me. Buck threw up at the sight.

"Who?" blurted Hardy.

From what I could tell, the pair looked to be a Black woman and a...suddenly, it hit me. "No! No!" I moaned.

In anger, I charged forward and cut the ropes with my Bowie knife. The bodies barely held together as they fell to the ground.

"Slave catchers!" cried Shorty.

Tears rolled from my eyes, and great sobs racked my body. How could they have done this? Why God? Why? Where was the antidote to this poison?

EPILOGUE

THE AMERICAN WESTERN frontier was mostly unforgiving, a meeting of savagery and civilization. The Texas Comancheria was wild country. By 1860, a few towns had begun to spring up. They served as bell-wethers to the civilizing of the frontier. *A Poison Spreads: Jack Seeks the Antidote* offers a peek into the courage, faith, endurance, and pure grit entailed in the conquest of the West. It presages the decades it would take to reap the bounty the region would eventually deliver. I had to deal with man's inhumanity to man and found my own faith tested as I pursued my mission to free slaves from bondage. Importantly, I had found a purpose to strive for that was greater than myself. But in this sequel to my tale, I first face seemingly certain death.

Life expectancy on the frontier was nothing like today. A male Indian did well to live beyond age thirty, and women could expect to live a tad less. Little wonder that older tribesmen were highly respected. Life expectancy for Whites wasn't much better. A White man on the frontier tended not to live beyond his late thirties.

Notably, the brevity of life generally meant that folks had to mature sooner. By the time a man or woman reached age fifteen or sixteen, he or she was pretty much an adult in terms of others expecting him or her to carry an adult set of responsibilities.

Dangers? Anthropology-minded folks claim there were as many as thirteen tribes of Comanche from the Quahadi or *antelope eaters* in the north to the Penateka or *honey eaters* in the south. Mix in Kiowa, Apache, and Tonkawa, and settlers had their hands full. The very name Comanche loosely translates in the Ute tribal language as *enemy*. Capture by the Comanche invariably led to terrible outcomes. A fearsome lot these tribes were. Notably, Penateka Comanche Chief Buffalo Hump led more than 600 warriors on a raid through the heart of Texas in August 1840, murdering Texans, looting the city of Victoria, and looting and burning Linnville on their march to the Gulf of Mexico. It was not until 1858 that Texas Ranger John Salmon *Rip* Ford led the force of 102 heavily armed Texas Rangers and 100 Indian allies that brought the Comanche to their knees at the Battle of Little Robe Creek on the Canadian River in Oklahoma as depicted in a previous Frontier Chronicle *Warpath: Jack's Faith is Tested*.

The northwestern plains were peopled by many tribes but especially the Sioux, comprised of three groups: Dakota, Nakota, and Lakota. My previous Frontier Chronicle *Hunted Vs. Hunted: Jack's Great Frontier Challenge* includes insights into the Lakota, in turn made up of seven subgroups: Oglalas (famed for Red Cloud and Crazy Horse), Hunkpapas (famed for Sitting Bull), Miniconjous, Oohenunpas (Two Kettles), Itazipacolas (Sans Arcs), Brulés (Burnt Thighs), and Sihasapas (Blackfeet). The Lakota history was no less combative than

Comanche or Cheyenne. Despite the violence of the frontier, it's worthy of note that the Lakota held to a worthy set of virtues, especially generosity, courage, fortitude, and wisdom. The North Platte country referred to in *A Poison Spreads: Jack Seeks the Antidote* was part of the Nebraska Territory that would eventually become Wyoming.

Oh, I do refer to bison as buffalo. Just for the record, bison and buffalo are quite different. Visualize the water buffalo and then the shaggy, awkward bulk of the American bison. Seems that *buffalo* came into common usage in America to refer to the bison, so I've chosen to use buffalo in my writings.

Historically notable in my Frontier Chronicles is that the longest and most used cattle trail was the Great Western Trail from 1874 to 1893. Thus, the trail I blazed in *Longhorns North* in 1857 and used in *Freedom Drovers* in 1859 presaged that route, following a course roughly a hundred miles to the west of the famed trail that ran from Matamoros, Mexico to Val Marie, Canada. As many as three hundred thousand cattle each year would eventually be driven up the Great Western Trail.

I enjoyed no modern creature comforts. Invention of telephones was decades into the future. Transportation? Horses, mules, and oxen—ridden or pulling wagons—were the vehicles of choice. I enjoyed no refrigerator to preserve sweet treats. There were no flush toilets or showers. Folks mostly ate what grazed upon or grew from the land. Learning was squeezed from the few books that might be found, especially the Holy Bible. Can't say that the living of the era was luxurious unless you counted the sheer grandeur of majestic landscapes and of nights so quiet you could hear the stars twinkling. To fully appreciate the place, you simply had to love the incredible beauty of the outdoors. Fishing the meandering Guadalupe River in Texas or the chill waters of Wyoming's North Platte River, hunting deer and antelope, raising cattle and horses, and reaping the bounteous yield of the rich soil was sheer joy for a courageous visionary few. For a teen on the frontier, life could be pretty good...mostly. Otherwise, it was downright dangerous.

Thus far, I had grown to manhood, conquered personal fears and prejudices, fought Indians and bandits, taken on prairie fires and storms, defended against wild beasts, traveled the wild country, driven cattle, found the love of my life, and settled upon a life purpose. As you have seen, I especially draw upon my faith and what I was taught by my parents. And yet, all of this is constantly tested. I had to learn to trust in instincts forged from my biblical and life lessons. Yes, I'm on a frontier adventure and more.

WATCH FOR DARKNESS LOOMS: JACK FACES WAR
(THE FRONTIER CHRONICLES 8)

COMING SOON FROM MARK GREATHOUSE

ACKNOWLEDGMENTS

Authoring books doesn't simply happen in a vacuum. The author provides the creative talent and crafts the stories, but there's so much more that demands acknowledgment. There are lots of folks and places that contribute to my authoring endeavors. So it is with *A Poison Spreads: Jack Seeks the Antidote*. The tale is set in 1860 and shares the trials and tribulations of a teen forced to meet the challenges inherent in the dangerous vastness of the western frontier, but this novel stands apart. At its core, it is also about the taming of that frontier. Step in two teen boys becoming men. The protagonist epitomizes the freedom of America's western frontier and represents a final bastion of honor in America. The tale follows Jack O'Toole's adventures in *Perilous Trails: Jack's Adventure Begins*, *Wyoming Calls: Jack's Risky Quest*, *Longhorns North: Jack's Great Trail Drive*, *Warpath: Jack's Faith is Tested*, and *Hunter Vs. Hunted: Jack's Great Frontier Challenge*. and *Freedom Drovers: Jack's Awesome Crusade*. Hopefully, readers will find *A Poison Spreads: Jack Seeks the Antidote* worthy of their time and emotional involvement.

I've been blessed with many friends and family who have supported my writings. My wife Carolyn's reviews and encouragement were a huge help, along with very important tech support from our sons Mike and Matt. Thanks to my nephew Shawn and pastor Randy for their faith insights. Many more friends and family have contributed support at some level to the creation and publication of my Frontier Chronicles, be it encouragement or advice.

Naturally, I am majorly grateful to the great folks at the Wise Wolf Books imprint of Wolfpack Publishing. The team they bring to publishing is first-rate in editing, cover design, and the myriad tasks that lead to successful book sales.

It's only right to acknowledge my ancestors who were actual settlers of the south Texas frontier. In addition to inspiring me, they provided a quite helpful true-to-life framework as to the life and times on the Texas Nueces Strip. It has been appropriate to weave them into the tapestry of my Western novels. Matthew Dunn (1815-1855) immigrated to Corpus Christi from County Kildare in 1845, established a homestead on Upriver Road, and served as a sutler to General Zachary Taylor's Army in the Mexican-American War. Peter Dunn (1807-1890) immigrated from Ireland in 1850 and established a blacksmith shop in Corpus Christi, John Dunn (1803-1889), my great great-great-grandfather, raised cattle and grew thousands of acres of cotton, Lawrence Dunn (1837-1864) fought and died with Captain Ware's Confederate cavalry, and my great-great-grandfather Nicholas Dunn (1835-1912) was a rancher, drover, livestock speculator, and Comanche fighter of some repute. My cousin John Beamond *Red John* Dunn (1851-1940) served as a Texas Ranger in the 1870s under Captain Bland Chamberlain (Company H), subsequently joined a *vigilance committee*, became a farmer and merchant, and curated a museum of military weapons displayed to this day in the Corpus Christi Museum of Science & History. Red John Dunn's brother Matthew Dunn also served as a Texas Ranger, and another cousin, Rut Evans, served as a Texas Ranger in the 1890s (Company E, Frontier Battalion, Alice, TX). My cousin Patrick Dunn was quite successful at raising longhorns on North Padre Island just east of Corpus Christi from 1883 to 1937. John Hillard Dunn (1883-1958), whose personal narrative about his family and his own adventures inspired my pursuit of my Texas family legacy, drove my own writings, and led me to write his yet-to-be-published biography *Tough Hombre—Recollections of a True Texan*. Finally, my grandfather, Horace Charles Greathouse served as a Texas Ranger in 1920 (Company C, Austin, TX). Such real-life characters, coupled with actual events have served to reinforce the historical settings for my writings. I've also personally walked the very landscapes traversed by my fictional and historical characters.

Most of my authoring has occurred in my office as decorated to channel my inner Texan, but my creative juices have often been inspired and imagination stoked in cafés and coffee houses across America. My favorites were Hester's Café & Coffee Bar in Corpus Christi, TX; Nueces Café in Robstown, TX; Java Ranch Espresso Bar & Café in Fredericksburg, TX; PAX Coffee & Goods in Kerrville, TX; Ragged Edge Coffee House and Bantam Coffee Roasters in Gettysburg, PA; 1889 Coffee House in Helena, MT; Dunn Brothers Coffee in Rapid City, SD; Postmasters Coffee & Bakery and Brio Coffeehouse in Waynesboro, PA; Birdie's Café and American Ice Co Café in Westminster, MD; Deja Brew Coffee House, New Oxford and Deja Brew at Miney Branch, Carroll Valley, PA; Baltimore Coffee & Tea Co., Frederick Coffee Company & Café, and Dublin Roasters in Frederick, MD; Qualle Café and Grounded Coffee & Bakery, Cherokee, NC; Palace Café, Amarillo, TX; and Unto Others Café, Lamar, CO. I must admit to also frequenting a few Dunkin Donuts and Starbucks around our fine nation.

The décors and easy-listening music in these fine establishments, combined with savory cups of coffee, tended to set me in the right creative frame of mind.

Last but not least, I'm especially thankful for the many folks who have read and enjoyed my books.

I do believe it's important to acknowledge how the Old West represents the brave pioneering spirit of settlers who met the challenges and transcended mere survival to enable America to achieve exceptional growth. The settling of the American frontier west is replete with tales of leveraging freedom for individual achievement. I hope you'll agree that reliving our past—even through history-based fiction—often has the effect of pointing the way to an ever-brighter future. Might we be up to it? I hope that the inspiration I've drawn from my having walked the very earth my characters have trodden, coupled with my extensive historical research, will enable readers to fully experience the grit, adventure, and passion of my characters while sensing aromas of gun smoke, trail dust, leather, and bluebonnets.

Thanks kindly to all of you and please do enjoy *A Poison Spreads: Jack Seeks the Antidote.*

ABOUT THE AUTHOR

 Award-winning author Mark Greathouse's love for the western genre draws upon his deep family roots and love of the outdoors honed from teen years hiking the Appalachian Trail and family travels across America's frontier. Greathouse began writing full time after a successful career as a business executive and later as an entrepreneurial investor and advisor. His service as president of several business and community nonprofits led to their extraordinary growth. He holds a BA in English and MBA in marketing. Greathouse donates time and books annually to support wounded military warriors.

A member of Western Writers of America and the Wild West History Association, he also contributes articles on the history of America's west to western-themed magazines. Greathouse was recognized as a 2024 Finalist in western genre by the American Literary Book Awards for his sixth Tumbleweed Saga, *Nueces Truth: Texans Face War's Realities*.

His *Frontier Chronicles*, a series of western novels aimed at adventure-minded teens and young adults while weaving a Christian message within their fabric, are aimed at lighting fires of truth, faith, hope, and life purpose in the bellies of today's teen boys and girls. Just as seeds must be sown to reap the harvest, so the seeds of faith must be planted to raise tomorrow's men and women.

GLOSSARY

DEFINITIONS

Bear sign—Cowboy slang for donuts.

Big Father or Great Father—All-powerful Indian deity.

Bota bag—A canteen fashioned from leather and popular among Indians, mountain men, and many travelers of the western frontier.

Cold Camp—Camp without a campfire, generally done to avoid the smoke that might alert threats.

Dog run—The sheltered space or breezeway between two sections of some southern ranch houses. Living quarters were usually on one side and sleeping quarters on the other.

Fletch—The fin-shaped bird feathers on an arrow that help stabilize its flight.

Gallery—A synonym for porch. Folks in the West often called them galleries.

Life debt—A cultural phenomenon in which someone whose life is saved or spared by another becomes indebted or in some way connected to their savior.

Pemmican—Lean dried strips of meat pounded into a paste, mixed with fat and berries, and then pressed into small cakes.

Possibles bag—A leather or canvas sack carried by cowboys and containing essentials like soap, matches, bandages, extra spurs, smoke makings, and playing cards

Remuda—A herd of horses frequently deployed on trail drives and by Plains Indians.

Shaman—Medicine man.

Teepee—An enclosed conical transportable shelter constructed of long poles and buffalo hides with a vent at the top to permit smoke to escape.

Travois—A wedge-shaped structure constructed of two poles and a cross-beam lashed together and dragged behind horses, mules, or dogs by Plains Indians.

———

COMANCHE TRANSLATIONS

Aitu—Not good

Ana o'a hi'it—Phrase for *desire to eat*

Ap—Father

Aruka—Deer

Eetu—Bow

Ekakwitsubaitu—Lightning

Ekapitu—Red

Eekasahpana paraiboo—Army officer (soldier chief)

Haa—Yes

Hawokatu—Hollow, loose

Hoikwa—Hunt, look for prey

Isa—Wolf

Isa wasu—Poison

Kaahaniitu—deceive, cheat

Kahni—Life

Kamakuna—Loved one

Kee—No

Kobe—Wild horse

Kohto—Build a fire

Kooitu—Die

Kuhmabai—Married

Kuisa—Coyote

Kuuna—Fire

Kuya akatu—Afraid of

Kwakuru—Defeat someone

Nahuu—Knife

Natsuitu—Strong

Numu—Cow, Cattle

Numunuu—Referring to the members of the Comanche tribes. Literally: people.

Ohapitu—Yellow

Onaa—Son or daughter

Paa—Water

Pabi—Friend

Paaka—Arrow

Peeka—Kill

Pia—Mother

Pia huutsuu—Bald eagle

Pia wa'óo—Comanche words for mountain lion, puma, or cougar.

Pihi—Heart

Pohya (or poya)—Walk

Puuka—Horse
Sunipu—Medicine (as in strong medicine)
Suumaru—Ten
Taa Narumi—Master; God
Tabu—Coward
Tamu—Rabbit
Tasiwoo—Buffalo
Tenahpu—Man
Tomoobi—Sky
Tosa—White man or woman
Tosaabitu—White
Tumah tuyai—After life
Tuhibitu—Black
Tumhyokenu—Believe, trust
Tu Taiboo—Black man
Umaru—Rain
Unha haksi nahniaka—Phrase for *what's your name?*
Wa'ipu—Woman
Wasápe—Bear
Wutsutsuki—Rattlesnake

LAKOTA TRANSLATIONS

Ate—Father
Ayústan—Abandon, retreat, leave
Igmuwatogla—Mountain lion
Isan—Knife
Iya Tate—Wind
Iyaya—Go, leave
Jiji—Light hair
Katá—Kill
Kize—Fight
Maka—The earth and grandmother of all things
Mato—Bear
Mini—Water
Nagi—The spirit that has never been a man
Niya—Ghost
Oyate—The people or nation
Sapa—Black
Ska—White
Scan—Sky

Sunkmanitu tanka—Wolf
Takuwe—Why
Tanka—Wolf
Tatanka—The great beast (patron of health, ceremonies, provision)
Unk—Created by Maka; embodies all evil beings
Unktehi—One who kills
Wakan tanka—God (monotheistic)
Wamaka nagi—Animal spirit
Wanbli—Eagle
Wani—Four winds (weather)
Wasake—Strong
Wash tay—Good
Wasichus—White man
Wasna—Pemmican
Wi—The sun (chief of all gods)
Wica—Complete man
Wicasa—Man (gender)
Wicasa wakan—Shaman
Winyan—Woman
Wowahwa—Peace
Zuzeca—Snake

www.ingramcontent.com/pod-product-compliance
Lightning Source LLC
Chambersburg PA
CBHW011434240626
47153CB00011B/2992